JADEN
POWERS

AND THE
INHERITANCE MAGIC

Also by Jamar J. Perry

Cameron Battle and the Hidden Kingdoms
Cameron Battle and the Escape Trials

JADEN POWERS

AND THE
INHERITANCE MAGIC

JAMAR J. PERRY

BLOOMSBURY
CHILDREN'S BOOKS
NEW YORK LONDON OXFORD NEW DELHI SYDNEY

BLOOMSBURY CHILDREN'S BOOKS
Bloomsbury Publishing Inc., part of Bloomsbury Publishing Plc
1385 Broadway, New York, NY 10018

BLOOMSBURY, BLOOMSBURY CHILDREN'S BOOKS, and the Diana logo are trademarks
of Bloomsbury Publishing Plc

First published in the United States of America in August 2024
by Bloomsbury Children's Books
www.bloomsbury.com

Bloomsbury books may be purchased for business or promotional use. For information on bulk purchases
please contact Macmillan Corporate and Premium Sales Department at specialmarkets@macmillan.com

Library of Congress Cataloging-in-Publication Data
Names: Perry, Jamar J., author.
Title: Jaden Powers and the inheritance magic / by Jamar J. Perry.
Description: New York: Bloomsbury Children's Books, 2024.
Summary: When his best friend Elijah disappears at a magical boarding school, Jaden uses his newly
acquired powers to find him and save the world from a sinister force that threatens to destroy it.
Identifiers: LCCN 2024002955 (print) | LCCN 2024002956 (e-book)
ISBN 978-1-5476-1278-9 (hardcover) • ISBN 978-1-5476-1279-6 (e-Pub)
Subjects: CYAC: Magic—Fiction. | Missing persons—Fiction. | Boarding schools—Fiction. | Schools—
Fiction. | Best friends—Fiction. | Friendship—Fiction. | Fantasy. |
LCGFT: Fantasy fiction. | Novels.
Classification: LCC PZ7.1.P44773 Jad 2024 (print) | LCC PZ7.1.P44773 (e-book) |
DDC [Fic]—dc23
LC record available at https://lccn.loc.gov/2024002955

Book design by John Candell
Typeset by Westchester Publishing Services
Printed and bound in the U.S.A.
2 4 6 8 10 9 7 5 3 1

To find out more about our authors and books visit www.bloomsbury.com and sign up for our newsletters.

To my inner child—
you made it through

JADEN POWERS

POWERS

AND THE
INHERITANCE MAGIC

CHAPTER ONE

"Where are you, Jaden?" Mama shrieked over the phone. *"It's five p.m.!"*

I sighed and rolled my eyes, my cell phone tucked near my right ear. "Mama, I'm at Elijah's house. I asked if I could come over here ... you know ... *this morning* before you left for work."

Elijah held a hand to his mouth to keep in his laughter as my mother yelled at me. Evening had come to Columbia Heights, the sun already beginning to drop behind the clouds. Elijah turned back to the television, his hands furiously pressing the game control buttons. I left him engrossed in *Assassin's Creed* and walked to his bedroom window that overlooked his small backyard. Row houses spread as far as I could see, bordering Elijah's house on the left and the right. I could just make out Adams Morgan in the distance, the neighborhood my mother was calling me from. Elijah didn't live that far from me, but with my mother's constant nagging, you'd think it was a hundred miles away.

"We told you to be home at five p.m.," Mama said, lowering her voice.

"You told me to be home at six p.m.," I corrected her.

"Jaden Powers, don't tell me what I said," she responded. "I know what I said, 'cause I was there when I said it."

I knew she would say that. She always did. I went to my text message screen, took a screenshot of our messages this morning, and sent it to her. "Check your phone. You told me six."

Mama quieted as the text message came through. There was a sharp intake of breath. "You're right. I'm sorry, Jaden. I've just been so . . . worried about you."

I sighed again. "I know, Mama, but I'm fine. You and Dad talk to me all the time about being safe and never staying out too late. And have I ever been late? I've always come home on time."

Her voice broke a bit. "We just care about you so much. We love you."

"And I love you. I'll be home in an hour, okay? Let me just say 'bye to Elijah."

I hung up before she could get another word in. My parents were always like that—hovering over me and being way too protective. They acted like I couldn't do anything. Okay, sure, I was a bit clumsy, and I wasn't the best at school or sports, but I at least knew how to tell time and when to come home.

2

Plus, I needed all the time I could get today. It was the end of summer, and school would start tomorrow. And Elijah would be going back to that fancy private school in Virginia. Without me.

"I sure wish you didn't have to go back to Hamilton," I grumbled, climbing into the bottom part of his bunk bed as he played the video game. "It's going to be awful around here without you. Especially dealing with the gremlins at home."

Elijah glanced at me and sighed, a sadness drifting through eyes that had turned glassy. But when I blinked, his tears were gone. He'd been like that all summer, growing sad whenever I mentioned Hamilton. Each time I pointed it out, he would shrug. I knew him enough to know he was hiding something, but when I asked about his secrets, he only went silent.

I decided to try again. "What are you thinking, Elijah? If you don't want to go back to Hamilton, just say it. What's been making you sad all summer?"

Elijah turned from me and snorted, his hands continuing to press his game controller buttons like they were the last buttons in the world. He began to mouth words, words I couldn't read. He did that sometimes, going absent-minded in the middle of conversations.

"At least the gremlins are actually around," he said, changing the subject. "My parents work too much. And going to Hamilton feels more like a prison than anything else." He glanced my way before turning back to his game. "It feels like prison wherever you're not."

A twinge of unhappiness pinched my chest. I felt the same way. My parents were always telling me I needed to have more than one friend and that it wasn't healthy to spend so much time with Elijah, but they didn't understand. Elijah was all that I needed.

Even though he came home every weekend, I took a moment to memorize him. His nose slanted downward, the tip of it upturned into a point. His eyes were round, the whites of them slightly red on the outskirts. His eyebrows were full and bushy, and there was a faded scar next to his temple. I had noticed it when he turned eleven, but he claimed he didn't know where it came from. His face was dark brown, like the midnight sky. I was lighter than him, but only slightly, my hair cut a bit closer on the sides than his. Elijah's mouth was set in a thin line, while my lips were full, protruded a bit, and you could see the slight gap in between my two front teeth when I smiled—which I quite liked. A blue jean jacket wrapped around his shoulders, the tops of it furred. Although his parents worked a lot, his clothing shone and smelled with a newness that mine didn't, and his shoes were as white as snow. I wore a brown hoodie and black jeans, and though I liked tennis shoes, it wasn't like I used them for much besides bicycling.

"What time is it?" Elijah said, bringing me out of my thoughts. He threw the controller down, stood, and stretched to the sky.

I checked my phone again. "Five ten."

He grinned. "Wanna go shoot some hoops before you have to leave?"

"You know I'm not good at that," I said, pulling the covers over my head.

4

I heard Elijah's shoes sink in the plush carpet as he approached and sat on the bed.

"Do you wanna talk about it?" he said.

"Talk about what?" My voice was muffled as I spoke through thick blankets. I could just make out the contours of his face through the rough, blue linen. Small hands grabbed my nose and wiggled it, soft laughter reaching my ears.

"You know *what*, Jaden," he said, pulling the covers from over my head. "Let's go outside before it's too late." I groaned, but I put on my shoes and followed him down three flights of brown, rickety steps, through the small kitchen with the white appliances, and to the backyard. If you could call it that. DC backyards were small and cramped, especially in Columbia Heights. Elijah's was bordered with a brown fence, the left side of it new with sleek wood, while the right was rotted in places, weathered by constant rain. A basketball hoop rose from the ground, its base a blue color. My bicycle stood near the back entrance, right next to the basketball.

Elijah picked it up in deft hands, bouncing it over the cracked pavement near the back door; he shot a three from where he was standing.

"*Whoosh*," he said, as the ball went through the net. I ran to pick it up and threw it back at him.

"Good job, Powers," he said, a smile lighting his face. "Quick on your feet."

"Yeah, quick to pick up your goals," I responded. I stood in front of him as he bounced the basketball, his lips opening again to mouth words. He moved so quickly that I could have sworn he disappeared in the breeze. I stuck out an arm to stop him, but it was for nothing. Warm wind ruffled my hoodie, and before I knew it, I heard the unmistakable sound of the ball going through the net again.

"Wait," I said, turning around to see Elijah spinning the ball on his index finger. "What happened? I didn't even see you!"

Elijah's eyebrow arched. "Maybe you just need to open your eyes."

I growled and went over to him again as he bounced the ball between his legs. He moved, and I noticed that he was mouthing words again. Time seemed to slow as I moved with him. My right arm rose, stopping him in his tracks, and I grabbed the basketball with my left. In a swift arch, I planted my feet, faked to the right, and then shot the ball above Elijah's outstretched hand, watching it sail across the pavement to the net, *whooshing* inside.

"I think I'm getting the hang of this," I said.

"So do I," he cheered, slapping fives with me. We played for the next ten minutes, but my momentary success at the beginning was the last. Elijah smashed fifteen shots in the goal to my two. And I had a feeling he gave me that second one.

"I gotta go," I said, checking my cell as he made the sixteenth shot. "It's five thirty."

"You're still not gonna say anything about me leaving?" he asked as I grabbed my bike from the fence.

"Nothing to say," I mumbled. "You're leaving for the year."

He grabbed my shoulders before I could jump on my bike. "I'll come home next weekend. We can hang out then. You know this."

"It's not the same as before you left," I said, folding my arms tight. "You get to go to your fancy school, and I have to start at Lincoln Middle tomorrow all by myself. The first day of seventh grade, Elijah. And you won't be there."

He fidgeted with his furred collar. "You know I don't have a choice," he whispered. "I gotta go, no matter if I want to or not. I can't control everything."

"Your parents do practically anything you ask them to. I'm sure you could convince them to let you go to Lincoln. I need you. Without you there, there's no one to talk to."

Elijah shifted from foot to foot, his gaze leaving mine. "If only it were that easy. There are things I need to do at school. I feel like it's too far gone now . . ."

"Too far gone?" I said, scrunching my eyebrows. "What the heck does that mean?"

"Nothing. You wouldn't understand, Jaden."

"Try me," I said.

"Just drop it," he said, returning his eyes to mine. "Just because I'm going back to Hamilton doesn't mean I don't want to be here with you. But it's the place where I'm meant to be."

"Just admit it. You'd rather be at your fancy school than with me, wouldn't you?"

He grew silent as he rubbed his neck, the tension so thick that it almost choked me. "You know that's not true, Jaden."

"Whatever."

His face grew angry now, and a coldness trickled through my hoodie, causing me to shiver, although the temperature was high. "Shouldn't you be going home?" he said, gesturing toward my bike.

I unfolded my arms and pushed his shoulders. Shock filtered through his expression. "I'll leave when you answer my questions."

Steel seeped through his tone. "Go. Home. Jaden."

We stood in silence for a while, the space between us so cold that I could almost see frost leaving my mouth as I breathed. When he didn't say anything else, I got on my bike, opened the gate, and cycled away without even saying goodbye.

I sent one more look his way and could just make out him bowing his head, his shoulders moving up and down as he cried.

CHAPTER TWO

Five days later, on Friday night, Daddy breezed into our house, briefcase in hand and tie askew. Mama, Austin, and I sat at the dining room table, eating salmon, jasmine rice, and broccoli.

"Shandra, good evening, my love," Daddy said playfully as he dropped his briefcase on the couch before going into the half bath near the kitchen to wash his hands. He worked as a trial lawyer at some big firm I couldn't remember the name of and was constantly late to dinner.

"Darius, good evening," Mama said, laughing loudly. She worked as a nurse, but her shifts started late at night most days. She watched me pushing pieces of my salmon around on my plate, impatient to get to Elijah's house. He should have been home from Hamilton by now. We'd texted each other apologies earlier that week, but I was still eager to see him and clear the air.

My brother, Austin, sat near Mama, stuffing his face full of fish and broccoli at the same time. A true disgrace. He was two years younger than me, but he acted like he was five instead of ten.

"Jaden, you're not hungry?" Mama asked me.

"He wants to go see Elijah," Austin said as he continued to stuff his face. Daddy took his seat at the farthest end of the table, uncovering the plate Mama had made for him.

"Close your mouth while you eat," I snapped.

"Speak nicely to your brother," she said. I stuck my tongue out at Austin when she wasn't looking. He grabbed his fork and jabbed it at me in a stabbing motion, a smile wrapping his face.

"May I be excused?" I asked.

"Not until you finish," Dad said.

I grumbled underneath my breath, but complied.

"Elijah's not going anywhere," Mama said. "Plus, you shouldn't be hanging around him so much anyway." I looked up long enough to see her glance at Dad. "You should be focusing on making friends who actually go to your school."

"Mooommmm," I whined while Austin snickered. "You already said I could spend the weekend with Elijah. He's going back to Hamilton on Sunday night."

Mama rolled her eyes and picked up the ever-present newspaper next to her plate, opening it to a random page. "Yes, I know what I said because—"

"*I was there when I said it.*" Austin finished her favorite saying for her, his glasses fogging up as he laughed.

"Anyway," Daddy said, changing subjects. "How was your first week of middle school?"

"It was fine, I guess," I grumbled, pushing the broccoli around my plate with my fork. School was the same as ever. I was always *okay* at everything but never good. Solidly middle of the pack. Not like Elijah, who got all As and started on all the sports teams.

"What about tutoring?" Mama said, which made me stiffen. "I emailed your principal requesting that you be paired with an eighth grader who could help you in math. I wasn't impressed with your grades last year."

"Tutoring is fine," I said. "I met with Jake the other day for help."

"And you don't have any homework for the weekend?" Dad asked, his left eyebrow arching.

"No," I lied, crossing my index and middle finger underneath the table. "I'm all done." Who cared if I had homework or not? Plus, Elijah would help me if I asked him to—he was good at everything.

Mama narrowed her eyes. "I'll believe it when I see it."

"I swear I'm done with everything. It's the first week of classes anyway, so the teachers won't give us too much to do until probably next week." I put on my best puppy dog face, and Mama's softened. "I promise. I got this."

"Okay," she sighed, returning her attention to her newspaper. "You're excused."

I raced to my room before she could change her mind,

running up the multiple flights of stairs and throwing open my door.

As I grabbed my sleeping bag from my closet, I couldn't help but wish Mama and Daddy weren't always so overprotective of me. I couldn't do anything fun without them always hounding me about homework, school, and chores. I wished they would just trust me a little bit more.

I took out my phone and sent a hurried text message to Elijah as I opened my backpack. **Dinner done. I'll be rushing to your house ASAP.**

I threw open my dresser, and tossed multiple T-shirts, shorts, and a light jacket inside, then ran into my bathroom to grab my toothbrush, shampoo, and body wash. Elijah always clowned me on the number of things I would bring, but I wanted to be prepared for anything.

"Did you have to bring your entire house?" he'd joke.

"You never know what you'll need," I'd always respond.

My phone hadn't vibrated yet. Elijah should have hit me back by now. *Hmm, that's weird.* I strolled back into my room, stuffing textbooks and notebooks inside my backpack. Maybe I *would* ask Elijah to help me with my homework.

The sound of clinking dishes from the kitchen and Austin blasting cartoons from the living room greeted me as I snuck down the stairs, holding my sleeping bag and backpack in a vise grip. Soft laughter reached me, a mixture of Dad and Mama's as they cleaned dishes together, and Austin's as he watched his favorite show. I checked my phone again—still nothing from

Elijah. I sent off another hurried text before going to the basement and opening the door that led to the backyard.

Coming now. It's the weekend!!!!

I unchained my bike and began the short trek to Elijah's house, my mind filled with ideas for what we could do together. Unlike my parents, Elijah's were rarely home. They didn't do long, drawn-out dinners like my family did. Elijah would just take his plate and eat in his room, or his parents would leave food for him when they had to work late. At my house, at least one parent was always present. Probably why I couldn't get away with *anything.*

My parents had asked me why Elijah almost never came over to our house, but why would I want that? At Elijah's house, we could stay up late, watch bad television, and eat as much candy as we wanted without my parents intruding.

My phone rang as I was cycling.

"Yes, Dad," I said.

"Did you make it to Elijah's okay?" he asked.

"I'm just around the corner. I'm not a baby," I whined.

"I'm just checking in," he said. "Make sure you call us when you get there; then call us tomorrow morning and Sunday, too. You got me, kiddo?"

"I gotcha."

He hung up as I was turning the corner onto Elijah's street and pulling into his front yard. Strangely, every light was off in his house, no brightness peeking through the blinds, in stark contrast to the other well-lit houses on the block. I clutched my hoodie close as a coldness seeped through it, a reminder that the end of summer came quickly to DC.

I climbed the flight of steps to the front door and rang the doorbell. I scrolled through my text messages while I waited, hoping to see something from Elijah, but there was nothing. I opened Instagram and navigated to Elijah's page to see if he had posted. The last photo was of us, posted a week ago, right before he was scheduled to go back to Hamilton. Frowning, I pressed the doorbell again and waited for five more minutes. No one answered. A couple walking their dog passed by, and I began to feel a bit ridiculous standing alone outside.

I walked my bike to the back of the house to see if his bedroom light was on. Like the front, it was just as dark, nothing stirring or moving. The fence looked menacing as the sun dipped behind the clouds, spikes poking into the sky like rigid snakes. I pressed Elijah's number, hoping he would pick up the phone; it rang once and then hung up. I shifted from foot to foot, my frustration growing. *What is going on?*

I returned to the front, but still nothing. No movement from the inside or outside.

My phone rang. Dad again.

"Yeah, I'm here," I said before he could say anything.

"Just wanted to make sure you were safe," he said.

"I'm coming home," I said.

"Wait, why?"

I shook my head. "No one's home. I've rung the doorbell multiple times."

Dad paused for a while before speaking again. "Hmm. That's weird."

"Yeah, I know. Dad . . ." I hesitated to ask the next question, my stomach burning with embarrassment. "You think he's mad at me? You know, for the other day?"

"Didn't y'all text about that argument and forgive each other?"

"We did, but what if he's still angry? What if he doesn't want to be my friend anymore?"

"Jaden, no need to start worrying yet. Maybe his parents haven't gotten home from picking him up from Hamilton, or maybe they decided to stay overnight. We don't know what happened."

I wiped a hand over my sweating forehead. "You're right. Okay, I'm coming back."

"Oh, no you're not," Dad said in a stern voice. "It's getting dark. I'll come pick you up. Wait for me on the steps and don't go in the street. You got me, kiddo?"

"Gotcha, Dad."

He hung up, and I sat on the steps and waited, resting my bike against my knees. He pulled up about five minutes later, stopping the all-black SUV right in front of me.

After he got out the car, he put the bike in the cargo space and helped me inside in the back seat, reaching to click my seat belt on.

"I got it, Dad," I said, fastening it myself.

"I can't care about my kiddo?" he said, smiling my way.

I rolled my eyes. "Let's just go."

He completed a fake salute and climbed into the driver's seat. "Your Uber awaits, my friend."

As he pulled away, I threw one more glance at Elijah's place. My heart jumped as the curtains on the second floor began to move. A dark shadow appeared as the curtains pushed aside, full curls falling on shoulders. The shadow was a familiar shape; I squinted and looked closer. Elijah's mother's face appeared in my line of vision.

I gasped.

It wasn't that she was standing at the window that surprised me.

It was the look of terror that drowned her face as she watched us drive away.

⌒

The smell of frying sausages, scrambled eggs, and French toast woke me the next morning. But the first thing I did was check my cell to see if there were any missed messages or calls from Elijah.

There were none.

I pressed the phone icon next to his name to give him a call, but this time there was no ring. No voicemail prompt. Nothing. Keeping my frustration at bay, I called his home number, but it didn't ring either. *Weird.*

I washed my face with hot water and threw on faded jeans and a too-large T-shirt before trudging down to the kitchen where Mama was reading the newspaper, and Dad was plating food with an apron around his waist.

"There he is," Mama said, standing and wrapping me in a warm hug, the scent of her soap wafting over me. "You slept in."

"It's nine a.m.," I said into her bathrobe. "That's late to you?" I tried to push away, but she held me even closer.

"No, no, just a few more moments," she said, which made me smile despite my aggravation. She did feel good, warm and inviting.

"Where's Austin?" I asked when she allowed me to sit down. Dad brought me a steaming plate of food.

"At your gram's for the weekend," Dad said, joining us. "She came to get him early this morning. You'd think he would've given us a hug before he left. Nope. He jumped in her car like he didn't care if he ever saw us again."

Toast stopped in my throat, causing me to cough.

"Baby, drink some juice," Dad said, gesturing to my cup.

I did as told, his words giving me pause as I thought about the last time I'd seen Elijah.

"I still haven't heard from Elijah, Dad," I said, placing my phone in the middle of the table to show them my text messages. "I've tried to contact him multiple times. He hasn't responded at all, and his phone isn't even ringing anymore. I'm starting to worry."

"I'm sure there's nothing to worry about, Jaden," Mama said. "I'm sure Elijah's fine. His parents just probably went to see him at Hamilton this weekend."

I narrowed my eyes. "That's the same thing Dad said last night."

She shrugged. "Because it's probably true." She sent Dad a loving smile. "We have the same mind, me and your dad. We know what we're talking about."

"Yeah, right," I whispered.

Dad cut his eyes at me. "Got something to say, Mr. Powers?"

"I'm just saying," I said, putting my fork down, "Elijah wouldn't just disappear like that, and not say anything to me. We're best friends! And I could've sworn I saw his mom looking out of their window last night when Dad came to pick me up! Which means she must have been in the house the whole time I was ringing the doorbell."

"Jaden," Mama warned. "Listen to us. Elijah is fine."

"Then explain this!" I said, pressing his number. It hung up as soon as I called it. I did the same to his home phone. "Either *no one* in his house has paid their phone bills, or something else is going on. I just know it. Elijah knew we were having a sleepover this weekend. We've texted about it all week!"

Dad sighed. "Jaden, mind your manners. Listen to us when we say that there's nothing to worry about."

"You guys never listen to me," I grumbled, stabbing my eggs with my fork. "I'm tired of it."

Mama's eyes flashed, and I could have sworn the room turned as cold as her stare. "Do you want me to take your phone for two weeks as punishment? Don't talk back to your parents."

I quieted, seething with rage. How was I supposed to find

out about Elijah if my own parents wouldn't help me or, heck, *believe me*?

Dad shifted his glasses. "Also, don't you think you need a few more friends anyway? Maybe see this as a blessing in disguise." He sent Mama another glance.

"Your dad's right. You spend so much time with Elijah you haven't made any friends who actually go to your school."

"You just don't understand," I whispered. "Something's wrong. And I don't want another friend."

They quieted now as I turned inward. After a few minutes of not eating, I spoke.

"Can I go to my room?"

"No, you need to finish your food," Mama said.

"You never listen to me!" I yelled, throwing down my fork and pushing back my seat to stand.

"Jaden," Dad warned. "Watch your mouth."

"Whatever," I said, anger erupting in my chest. "I'll just stay in my room since this is a dictatorship!"

With that, I turned on my heels and ran upstairs, slamming the door behind me.

CHAPTER THREE

I stayed in my room into the evening, ignoring my parents' knocks on the door. Mama stopped by multiple times, saying, "Jaden, we don't like when you don't speak to us. We need to know you're at least okay."

"I'm fine," I managed to say before I turned back to the book I was reading.

When they were gone and hadn't returned for a couple of hours, an idea popped into my head. If they weren't going to check in on Elijah, then I would. I threw on a jacket and tiptoed downstairs, stopping by my parents' room. The sound of their television was loud, convincing me that they wouldn't hear. I snuck down the rest of the stairs and grabbed my bicycle by the front door, pressing in the code to silence the alarm system so it wouldn't send my parents running.

The wind was warm as I biked over to Elijah's house, my mind filled with all types of horrors I might find when I got there. What could have happened to Elijah? And why had his mom been staring out of the window, ignoring the many times I'd rung the doorbell? It just wasn't like Elijah or his mom to ignore *me* of all people. And it wasn't like Elijah not to message me back. And what was going on with their phones? All these mysteries ran through my mind as I maneuvered back to Elijah's place, my heart hammering in my chest.

His home looked much like it did before, dark and uninviting, the driveway in the back empty of cars. It even *felt* empty, stark and cold, like no one had ever lived here before. I gazed into the windows, hoping beyond hope that I would see something, anything. But the curtains didn't stir like last time, as if Elijah's mother had been a ghost.

"Jaden, don't do it, don't do it," I pleaded with myself before jumping off my bike. "Okay, just do it." I moved behind the house, focusing my attention on Elijah's closed window on the second floor overlooking the backyard. After settling my bike against the fence, I looked for spaces in the grooves of the bricks I could use to hoist myself up. When the fear made me shiver, I decided to just pick up clods of dirt near the basketball hoop and throw them at his window.

There was nothing, no movement in the curtains, or sounds. Just me looking like a clown throwing dirt clods. I picked up a few more and threw them, but still nothing.

"Well, that didn't work. Time to climb." I took a deep breath and strolled over to the bricks, preparing to begin an ascent to Elijah's bedroom.

I paused for a second. *Wait, that's not a good idea.* I didn't want to be on the news as the preteen Black boy who broke into someone's house. I wouldn't have an easy explanation for that.

Sadness gripped me as I returned my attention to the window, about to return home. But a sudden light stopped me in my tracks. It was coming from Elijah's bedroom. It seemed like . . . fire . . . more than anything else, flickering in and out, a mixture of different shades of oranges, yellows, and blues. When I squinted to peer closer, smoke wafted into the air, climbing toward the ceiling, causing me to stumble back in fear. I stifled a scream and blinked once. The fire and smoke disappeared.

What? That didn't make any sense.

My phone rang, *loudly*, and I jumped. I checked my phone to see a text message from Mama.

Get home. Now.

Jaden, you've really gotten yourself in trouble now.

That thought reverberated in my mind as I pedaled home. I just knew Mama and Daddy would ground me for life; not only had I argued with them this morning, but I had also snuck out *and* nearly broken into somebody's house.

But I had to. They weren't listening to me. They never did.

I half expected police lights and blaring alarms as I turned onto my street. But there was only Elijah's parents' familiar Honda Accord parked on the side street in front of our house. The front door opened as soon as I stopped, Mama and Daddy coming outside, dressed in nightclothes.

"Come inside," Mama said, putting her arms around me. The porch light illuminated tears glistening in her eyes.

"I'm sorry," I said, picking up my bike and going up the stairs. "I just had to go back to Elijah's house. I didn't mean to make you upset."

They both draped me in warm arms. "It's okay, Jaden," Daddy said. "We just need you to come inside."

"What's going on?" I said, pulling back.

"Just come inside, baby," Mama repeated. "Elijah's parents need to talk to you."

I did as I was told and found Elijah's parents in the living room, his mother pacing back and forth, running trembling brown hands through her hair. His father stood near the mounted television set, looking as if he hadn't slept in days— his clothes were rumpled and his hair was unkempt.

"Mr. and Mrs. Williams, what's going on?" I asked again. "Is this about Elijah?"

"How about you sit down, son?" Mr. Williams said.

"Will someone tell me what's going on?" I said, sitting on the gray sectional as my parents and Mr. and Mrs. Williams surrounded me. Dad put a hand on my shoulder, rubbing and then pressing down. My heart was beating so hard that I thought it would jump out of my chest. "I know what I did was wrong, okay? I didn't mean to leave without permission. I was just trying to see if Elijah was home or not. It's not like him not to text or call me back. And then I checked his Instagram and—"

"We're not mad at you, Jaden," Mrs. Williams said, kneeling in front of me. "I saw you yesterday. I . . . I just didn't know how to tell you. Please forgive me. I—I was a coward." She grabbed both of my hands, but then released them and went back over to her husband, crying into his shoulder.

My heart stopped. "What—what happened?"

I knew the answer before even asking the question. I knew it because no one was angry with me. But I needed them to say it, to put all my fears into words. Even though I knew what was coming next.

"What happened to Elijah?" I whispered.

Mr. Williams cleared his throat. "He—he's gone. I'm so sorry. He's gone. He died yesterday."

His words washed over me like thunderous waves. My fingers began to tremble as I stared at them. How? How was this real life? Not Elijah. Not my best friend. It couldn't be. It couldn't be that he wouldn't be coming back. Wouldn't be coming back to me.

The room grew silent for a long while besides the small sobs from Mrs. Williams.

"What happened?" I finally said after what seemed like hours.

"An accident," Mr. Williams said.

Daddy kept rubbing my shoulders while Mama sat next to me on the couch, pulling me into an embrace. "It's going to be okay, Jaden. We're right here with you."

"What kinda accident?"

"He drowned. I'm so sorry, son," Mr. Williams said.

I stared daggers into Mr. Williams's eyes, which made him flinch a bit. "Elijah was amazing at swimming though."

Mr. Williams continued, clearing his throat. "He was at his grandmother's house in Georgia before heading back to school. He was swimming in the pond next to her house, and when he was gone for too long, his grandmother went searching for him." His voice hitched in his throat as he finished the story, tears leaking from his eyes now. "She found his body washed up on the shore."

"That—that can't be true," I whispered, but a hole was forming in my heart. I clutched my chest as a pain settled there. My breath started to come out in ragged streams. Not Elijah. Not like this. "He—he said he hated going to his grandmother's house in the summer. He told me he was going back to Hamilton. Why would he go there?"

"We made him go," Mrs. Williams said. "We thought it would be good for him to see her and his cousins. You know how Elijah is—I mean, *was*—you and he were inseparable. He would go to Hamilton and then would come home talking about seeing you. He never talked about making friends at school, and we just wanted him to get some distance, to find himself. DC was just not a place for him to do that."

"So, your solution was to send him to the place where he died?"

"Jaden, please," Mama said. "They're hurting as much as you are."

"Mama, I just want to be alone," I said, standing, tears starting to rain down my face like a water faucet. "Please, please, just for tonight." I half expected them to tell me to sit down and listen to reason. But she only nodded and turned her face from mine. She had started crying too.

I needed to get away, to get away from the sorrow, to come to terms with the fact that my best friend wasn't coming home. That I would never see him again.

I ran up the stairs and slammed my bedroom door. When I buried my face in my pillows, I couldn't help but scream and scream, tears soaking my clothes and bedding.

Elijah was gone, and there was nothing I could do about it.

CHAPTER FOUR

I sat in my room all night, drifting in and out of sleep, my mind playing back all the good times I'd had with Elijah, from when we'd first met in the first grade, to us swimming in the neighborhood community center's pool, to him inviting me to his house to play video games, to the many vacations I'd invited him on with my family over the years.

We'd been inseparable, and now I'd never see him again.

Elijah couldn't be dead. He just *couldn't* be.

It wasn't until five o'clock in the morning that my mind turned from the past to the present. I sat upright in my bed as the realization hit me.

Something was *off*. Strange. Weird.

Everything Elijah's parents had told me about his death wasn't making sense. They'd said they sent him to his grandmother's house, but Elijah had told me that he was heading back to Hamilton. Elijah was always upfront with me, and absolutely hated lying. So, why would he tell me he was going to Hamilton when his parents were sending him to his grandmother's house? That made no sense.

Also, Elijah and I had swum hundreds of times at the community center. Our parents had been adamant that we learn how to swim at an early age so we wouldn't fear it as adults. He was the strongest swimmer I knew, so how in the world had he drowned in his grandmother's pond? The slow currents in it were child's play to Elijah.

I gasped aloud as my mind whirred with another thought. I had seen that bright flame in Elijah's bedroom earlier, along with the smoke drifting to the ceiling. I wasn't filled with grief when I'd seen that, so I *knew* my eyes weren't playing with me.

"Someone has to be lying," I said aloud to the darkness. "Elijah can't be dead."

My parents found me a grief therapist after Elijah died. I refused to talk to her though.

I was convinced Elijah was still alive.

I sat in the back seat of Dad's car the next Saturday after a challenging session, scrolling through Elijah's Instagram profile, my mind going over the events of the last few days. I couldn't stop thinking about the light and smoke I saw in his bedroom. Why were they there? I wanted to go back to his house, but his parents had probably already packed his belongings away.

"You know I only want what's best for you, right?" Dad said from the driver's seat.

"Yes, Dad," I said.

Even though the car was loud, I could still hear him sighing.

"I know that this is a hard pill to swallow, losing your best friend and all. But Elijah's gone and you have to talk about it."

"I don't want to go back to therapy," I said.

Dad's voice turned hard. "You don't have a choice, kiddo. Your mom and I have booked you an appointment every Saturday morning for the foreseeable future."

"I never get a say," I muttered.

His eyes flashed to me before glancing back at the road. "What was that?"

"Nothing, Dad."

After a while, he pulled into the McDonald's on Georgia Avenue next to Howard University. It was usually packed, but today was semi-quiet. We went through the drive thru where Daddy ordered two ice cream cones before parking and leading me to the benches near the road. He handed me a cone, and we ate in silence for a while, but I couldn't help my eyes lighting up at the sugary sweet. This was me and Dad's thing, but we hadn't done it in a few months. It was a time where we could just . . . be . . . just me and him.

"I wish . . . ," Dad began to say before his voice caught in his throat.

"Don't," I said, my eyes welling up. "I don't want to cry anymore."

"I can't help it," he responded, wiping his eyes. "You shouldn't know what death is yet. I wanted you to finish school and go to college and live your life for a while before all of this."

"It's okay."

But it wasn't. It would never be, not without Elijah by my side. I didn't want to lose him, but I was convinced I *hadn't* lost him; I just had to find the proof I needed.

Dad finished eating his cone and threw the wrapper in the trash can beside us. "Elijah's parents reached out. His memorial is tomorrow. It's your choice to go or not."

That was it! I needed to get back inside Elijah's house again. I just *knew* I could find the evidence I needed to locate him, or at least a piece of the puzzle.

I cleared my throat as I chucked my wrapper into the trash can.

"Perfect shot," Dad said. "Basketball player in your future?"

I grinned. "Absolutely not. That was Elijah's lane."

"So what do you think, kiddo? Are you up for it? I'm sure we can think of something else to do to celebrate Elijah's memory if you don't want to go."

"I wanna go," I said, gulping. "He was my only friend. My best friend."

He got up and wrapped warm arms around me as I leaned into him. He smelled of a mixture of aftershave, sugar, and beard oil. "I got you, Jaden. You know that, right? We're going to get through this together."

I memorized every inch of him, hoping and wishing that I would never lose my family.

"I know, Dad."

CHAPTER FIVE

Grievers and mourners filled Elijah's house as I stepped inside while holding Austin's hand. He was surprisingly quiet today, which made sense. Elijah used to always tell Austin that he was like the little brother he never had. Austin and I were dressed alike, wearing white dress shirts, suit jackets, black pants, penny loafers, and red ties.

The living room was packed, church shoes sinking into carpets, the smell of peppermints overwhelming. A gigantic picture of Elijah stood on an easel near the fireplace, his hair perfectly cut, a huge smile on his face. I remembered when he had posed for that picture, part of family photos from last year. People passed by the photograph, some crying, some touching it reverently, and some whispering quietly to each other. The Williamses stood by the picture, all tears gone from their faces. I imagined that they had to be all cried out after this week. An older woman stood near Mrs. Williams, the spitting image of Elijah.

My heart hitched. That had to be his grandmother from Georgia.

People continued to pass by, touching their hands, whispering calm reassurances to them.

Dad and Mama walked into the house after us. "Go ahead and pay your respects, boys. Elijah would have wanted that," Mama whispered.

Austin pulled my arm. "Will you go with me?"

"Of course I will, little bro."

Austin sniffed as we got in line. After a short while, we were standing in front of the Williamses. I held out the apple pie Mama had baked for the memorial.

"Mama made this." I couldn't figure out what else to say.

Elijah's grandmother reached out and touched the box. "That was nice of her," she said, her eyes finding mine.

Mrs. Williams reached out to me, holding me close to her. "I know you loved him."

When she let me go, Austin handed over a box of Uno cards to Mr. Williams. "He gave me these the last time he spent the night at our place. Make sure they're . . ." He burst into tears and ran back to Mom before he could finish.

"How about you put the pie in the kitchen?" Mr. Williams suggested to me.

I nodded. As I made my way to the kitchen, Mr. Williams cleared his throat and the room silenced.

"We want to thank everyone for showing up today. Showing up for Elijah. He deserves it and so much more. As you all know, Elijah was a great kid, a blessing to us all. He always succeeded in . . ." Mr. Williams paused and coughed, so Mrs. Williams took over.

"He always succeeded in school," she finished for him. "We knew that Hamilton was the best place for him to be, especially since he showed great promise at such an early age. We just hate that his life ended so tragically. No mother or father should go through the loss of a child. Especially a child like Elijah. Again, we thank all of you for coming, and especially Jaden, his best friend." She pointed to me holding the pie. When everyone turned to me, I immediately got nervous and twitchy. "Thank you, Jaden, for showing Elijah what true friendship is all about. You were with him since he was a little boy. Now we get to see him in you as you grow up."

That made me a bit uncomfortable, especially since I knew something was off. One thing I did know was that I couldn't stay in this living room anymore, not with his parents giving a speech about how great Elijah was and not after seeing that big picture staring at me from the easel at the front of the room. I gripped the apple pie in steel hands and walked into the kitchen.

The table was piled high with food, and my nose was drawn to a long pan covered with aluminum foil, smelling of baked macaroni and cheese. My stomach bubbled at the scent of baked chicken, green beans, and mashed potatoes, and at the sight of dinner rolls dribbled with butter on top. But an idea came to me as I stood there. While everyone was out there memorializing Elijah, I could take this time to go searching in his room.

After placing the apple pie on the kitchen table, I jogged upstairs to Elijah's room. It hadn't changed at all since I was last here; it was still messy, his bed was still unmade, and the controllers we were just using for gaming were strewn on the floor, the cords from both mixed up with each other. It didn't look as if his parents had even attempted to come inside since they delivered the news. I narrowed my gaze and tiptoed around the room as I looked for the firelight and smoke again, but I couldn't see anything. Had I been imagining them?

I sat on the bed to think. Maybe Elijah really was dead. Maybe I needed to find a way to let him go while keeping his memory alive.

The tears came now. They leaked from my eyes like a thunderstorm, coming down like rain. I took off my shoes and lay on his pillow, closing my eyes as the tears fell. My hand brushed against something hard. *Wait, what was that?* I sat up to find a yellow spiral notebook sticking out from underneath Elijah's pillow. A loose sheet of paper fell to the bedcover when I opened it.

With timid hands, I picked both up. Words were scrawled across the notebook pages, but they were indecipherable to me, written in another language. It wasn't any language I was even slightly familiar with; the words were set in boxes, with symbols

I couldn't recognize, star shapes, and circles. It actually reminded me of the weird aptitude tests that my school used to determine the gifted students. However, the language on the pages was set like real writing, scrolling from left to right, from the top to the bottom.

"What is this?" I whispered as I sifted through the notebook. When I went back to the loose sheet, though, I noticed that the top line had deep blue letterhead, and it was in English!

THE FIVE EMERGENCES SCHOOL OF MAGIC
PROPERTY OF ELIJAH WILLIAMS

I read the words aloud, confused and disoriented a bit. What did this mean? *The Five Emergences?* What was that? And how did it connect to Elijah?

Whatever it was, this notebook belonged to Elijah. For some reason, it made me feel closer to him now that he wasn't with me. Emotion welled in me as I stared at it. A tear dropped from my right eye, splashing against the loose page. *Oh, crap.* I didn't want to deface anything Elijah was working on.

I gasped. The words on the page had just lit up, as though they were tinged with fire! As I watched, they started to move, rearranging on the page until they became readable:

Jaden, I'm sorry I had to leave, but something's gone wrong.
A horrible evil is after me.
I need your help.

I threw the notebook and paper across the room and screamed so loudly that I was sure that everyone at the memorial downstairs had heard me. Fear gripped me to the point that I was shaking, my breath blowing in ragged streams.

I closed my eyes, willing my racing heart to calm. "It's okay, Jaden. It's okay."

With a heave, I stood, opened my eyes, and picked up the notebook and paper before returning to the bed, reading the words on the loose sheet again.

The words were in Elijah's handwriting. *I knew it!* I knew he was alive, and this page was my evidence.

"But how did this happen?" I whispered aloud as I glanced from the spiral notebook to the loose sheet of paper. "Did I just . . . change the words on my own? Did I do this? And how am I supposed to help Elijah?"

I didn't know where to start, but I would do anything and everything to help him like he asked.

Without thinking, I stuck the loose sheet inside the notebook, put it into my suit jacket, and made to stand and go back to the memorial. A sharp pain exploded behind my eyes, tracing along my forehead. Light flashed across my vision, leaving me blind and clutching my head. A soft scream escaped my mouth, even though I wanted to yell as loudly as possible. My knees fell to the floor with a sickening *crunch*, the pain in my head so bad that I couldn't stop myself. Shivers racked my body as I fell to my side, convulsing to the point that I thought I would die. Saliva dripped from my mouth, pooling in a puddle under my cheek.

"No," I managed to moan.

The agony took over, leaving me with no words to say, no screams to yell, only shakes and convulsions.

Sweet bliss finally took over, and I fell unconscious.

_c_

Voices found my ears when I came to, although my vision was still impaired.

"Do you think he's okay?" It was Mama's voice, soft and pleading. I tried to move my lips, but no sound came.

"I think he's fine." Dad's voice now, deep and nervous. "He probably passed out here after sneaking up to Elijah's room. Probably hasn't slept in days."

"We should leave," Mama said. "I don't want Elijah's parents finding us up here."

"What about Austin?"

"I'll get him."

Dad put my shoes on and picked me up, holding me close in his big arms. He carried me downstairs, through the kitchen and outside to his SUV where he settled me in the back seat, kissing my forehead while he strapped me in. "It's going to be okay, Jaden. I'm here with you."

After a while, Mama got into the car, putting Austin in his seat. He was asleep too, at least from what I could tell, considering he wasn't doing his constant jabbering.

My vision slowly returned as we drove down the road back home. My head pounded as I tried to figure out what just happened to me in Elijah's room. Voices churned in my head, a jumble of sound that made no sense to me just yet, not until Mama started talking.

I hope Jaden is okay with everything that's going on.

I blinked once and saw Mama turn to Dad and shift his collar where I could clearly see her mouth not moving, even though I heard her speaking once again.

Elijah meant so much to Jaden. I just hope that Elijah's death doesn't ruin his life.

Did I just—did I just hear Mama's thoughts?

Mama turned to me now, her eyes finding mine, growing wide.

"Jaden, are you okay? What happened in Elijah's room, baby?"

I jumped so high that my head brushed against the ceiling.

"Jaden, what's wrong?" Dad called from the front seat, his eyes still on the road.

"I think I just heard—" I managed to say before my hands moved involuntarily. Flame burst from my fingertips as Mama screamed. A cobalt light flashed across my hands and hit me in the chest, which was as painful as you would think.

Boom!

The light *exploded*, and everything happened all at once. Austin woke up from his seat screaming, Mama joined, the light from my chest expanded and shot to the front of the car, Dad swerved the wheel like it had a mind of its own, and then the car veered to the left, slamming into the road guardrail.

The heavy sound of metal on metal screeched together,

drowning out our yells of terror. My hands—which had returned to normal—flew to my ears to drown out all sound while flame and smoke lurched into the sky from the flown-open hood of the car.

In a split second, Mama opened her door and jumped out, dragging Dad with her. In another, Austin was dragged out too, and then Mama undid my seat belt and pulled me to safety. We all stumbled to the side of the road, cars on the highway swerving out of the way.

The SUV's left side was smashed into the guardrail like a pancake. Flame shot upward and smoke clogged the air. Mama pulled me into her arms and placed her jacket around my mouth while Dad did the same for Austin.

We stood there for a while, looking at the car wreck, shocked.

I gazed at my hands and then at my chest.

What did I just do?

CHAPTER SIX

The police arrived after Dad made the call, and they asked him questions while they wrote their report. I couldn't help but catch the disbelief and shock in Mama's eyes.

There was no need to figure out what had just happened because I knew the answers. Somehow, I had heard Mama's thoughts, and the next moment, *I* had caused the accident. Was I magical? Did I have some hidden power that I hadn't known about until now?

One thing was clear to me though. Elijah was *not* dead. And the only one who would know how to help me was probably him.

But where in the world was he?

Dad came back to us after the police called a tow to come get the SUV.

"We should get home," he said, calling an Uber from his phone. The tow truck and the Uber came at the same time, and we watched as our car was hitched to the tow as we rode away. I sat in the back of the rideshare, holding on to Austin, who wouldn't stop sniffling. I felt so bad about what had happened, but I couldn't control it. I was even starting to believe that I'd imagined the whole thing until I noticed that the hand that held on to Austin's shoulder was starting to glow again with that ethereal light. I placed both hands in my suit jacket as we pulled into our driveway.

It began to rain, matching my gloomy feelings as Dad wrapped Austin in his arms and carried him in the house, leaving Mama and me to go inside together.

My heart pounded as I thought about everything that had happened. Should I tell my parents the truth? But no, they wouldn't believe me anyway. I wasn't sure if I even believed myself.

Magic doesn't exist, Jaden, they'd probably say. I wanted to tell them everything, but they had already shown me over the years that, although they loved me, they would never listen long enough to believe me.

I was going to have to find everything out on my own.

"I . . ."

"What?" Dad asked, as he came from upstairs.

"Nothing," I said, sighing. "I'm going to bed."

I couldn't help but hear Mama's soft sobs as I went upstairs and closed my bedroom door.

Lightning struck outside my window as the rain turned to a torrent. Barely paying attention to it, I took off my suit jacket and spread the spiral notebook and the loose sheet on my desk, turning on the lamp to examine them.

The pages inside the notebook were frozen in that same indecipherable language, but the loose sheet still had Elijah's words on it, calling me to help him. I noticed my teardrop had smudged the ink a bit. My heart dropped as the water stain on the page leaped into the air, growing into a huge water bubble. A large scroll appeared in its depths before the bubble burst, spraying water all over my head, soaking me from head to feet.

"Hey!" I screamed angrily. But the only response was the large scroll *thwacking* my right shoulder as it fell, pain lancing to my chest. I squeezed out my wet shirt, picked up the scroll, and opened it on my desk with a *whoosh*.

My heart beat so loudly as I pored over the page and read aloud.

THE FIVE EMERGENCES
HEADMASTER: SIMEON CARMINE

Jaden Powers, first of his name, is hereby invited to attend The Five Emergences School of Magic to learn to become a Sorcerer.

As you have probably guessed by now, you have had your first Outburst, manifesting a power that you cannot yet understand.

And no, you are not a witch or warlock!

Rest assured, The Five Emergences will train you in everything you need to know to fulfill your duties as a Sorcerer.

The Five Emergences requests your presence at a Wand Bonding ceremony and invites you into its coveted ranks as a Sorcerer.

Do you Accept or Reject?

Take a wand and touch one of the boxes below.

Please note: If you decide to Reject, your memory will be erased, and your magic will disappear. Or you will die.

We don't know which will happen.

Everyone is different.

ACCEPT ☐   REJECT ☐

A *wand*? Where the heck was I supposed to find a wand?

Boom. Lightning struck outside my window again. I grabbed the scroll, ran to the window, and peered out; my eyes were blinded for a second before they adjusted to the brightness. I gasped when I saw what was in front of me.

Lightning had struck the street, but it hadn't disappeared—it was frozen in place like someone had pressed the pause button on it. Even the rain had paused; it looked like needles had fallen from the sky and stopped in their tracks.

"Mom? Dad?" I yelled. No response. I opened my bedroom door and went to the second floor to Austin's room. He was asleep in his bed, covered in his Spider-Man sheets, but there was something different. His mouth was opened in a loud snore, but the sound pierced the silence nonstop, and he wasn't taking a breath.

What the—

The doorbell rang, loud and deafening.

I snuck to the top of the stairs, leaning over the railing. "Mom? Dad?" Still nothing.

The doorbell rang again, this time louder than the first, so loud that I had to place my hands over my ears. Whoever it was, they were *not* leaving.

I went downstairs to find Mama and Daddy frozen just like Austin. Dad was sitting on the couch yawning with his arms outstretched, and Mama was standing with the television remote in her hand. I waved my hands over their faces, but they didn't move. The doorbell rang once again, and, this time, a deep voice sounded through the door.

"You might want to let me in, Mr. Powers. You won't be able to press the 'Accept' or 'Reject' box without my help, you see. And I'm afraid your parents and brother will remain frozen until you make your choice." The voice was kind, but authoritative.

"How do I know I can trust you?" I had begun to shake now.

"Because I'm the only one who can help you now," the voice said.

Could this person know about Elijah? Was Elijah a Sorcerer too, like the invitation said I was? Unfortunately, I couldn't answer those questions without letting the person in who was ringing my doorbell. *Jaden, what have you gotten yourself into?*

With shaky hands, I opened the door to find a large man standing on the doorstep, smiling a pleasant smile. A strange-looking octagonal hat, etched with a stitching of unicorns, sat on his head, and a black cape was wrapped around his shoulders. His skin tone matched mine. He wore black pants with buckles lining the entire fabric, all the way from his boots to his belt. His vest changed colors every time he moved, from orange to pink to blue to black and then other colors that I didn't have a name for. An umbrella was in his hands, but it was completely dry.

"May I step in? We have much to discuss."

I folded my arms. "First, tell me who you are."

He did an elaborate bow. "I'm Professor Simeon Carmine, Headmaster of The Five Emergences School of Magic."

The school from the invitation and Elijah's note! The invitation scroll was still in my hands, the man's name etched at the top of it.

"Okay, come in," I said, stepping aside. Professor Carmine entered and looked around the house, smiling as he did.

"Ahh, the illustrious Powers residence."

"It's okay, I guess."

He went to my frozen parents and appraised them, whispering to himself. "Hmm. Everything seems to be in place. Looks like the vision I had when you had your Outburst."

"The invitation mentioned an Outburst. What's that, Professor . . . Carmine, you said? Did I have one?"

Carmine blinked. "Oh. You know nothing. About anything."

I huffed. "Is that a crime?"

"Not a crime. We have students who come from the normal world all the time. They just tend to have their Outbursts at a younger age."

My questions came in rapid-fire succession. "What are Outbursts? What happened to my parents? What happened to Elijah? Did he have magic? Wait, do *I* have magic now? What is going on?"

Carmine put up both hands. "Wait, slow down. One question at a time."

I took a breath. "Is my family okay?"

"Just a formality. We must protect the magical world from the non-magics. And we must protect the non-magics from the magical world. They'll unfreeze when you make your decision."

"What are Outbursts?"

Carmine took out what looked like a thick black stick and waved it in the air, muttering in a language that I had never heard before. An image appeared, the scene of my parents' SUV smashed into the guardrail.

"*Tsk, tsk, tsk.*"

"Wait!" I said, pointing at it. "That happened just today, right when we were leaving . . ." I gulped. "So, I did do that?"

"That's precisely what an Outburst is," Carmine responded.

"A spontaneous combustion of magic. It usually starts with telepathy and then ends in a destructive spell. It shows that *you* are magic, Mr. Powers. Meaning that you are a Sorcerer."

I jumped a bit. "I heard my mom's thoughts before I crashed our car!"

Carmine smiled. "The one and only time you'll be able to do that, I'm afraid. How old are you?"

"I'm twelve."

A look of confusion traced Carmine's face. "Hmm . . . that's certainly strange."

"Strange how?"

Carmine shook his head as the image disappeared. "More on that later. But an Outburst is an explosion of magic that happens when a Sorcerer comes of age. It's the one and only time you can use your power without a wand. After that, you must be bonded with one. Once I detect an Outburst, I send a professor from The Five Emergences to meet the prospective student. I decided to come myself for you. Would you like to Accept or Reject our invitation?"

"But wait," I said. "What is this place? And what am I supposed to learn there?"

Carmine drew himself to his full height, his head brushing against the ceiling, a proud tone entering his voice. "Why, The Five Emergences is an illustrious magic school, my boy. The one and only in our universe. Where students come to learn, practice, and use all manner of magic. You'll learn to become a Sorcerer there, a being of immense power."

I took a step back. "I was *right*. There *is* something else going on here. Did you know Elijah? Elijah Williams?"

Carmine blinked again and shook his head. "That name doesn't ring a bell."

I couldn't tell if he was lying or not.

"So, I'm a Sorcerer? I can do magic?"

Carmine began to pace. Oddly, his movements made no noise. "Precisely. But after your Outburst, you cannot complete a spell without a wand."

"Where do I get one of those?"

Carmine laughed at that, the sound filling the entire house. "My dear, you cannot just *get* one of those. One has to *bond* with you." He brandished the black stick again. "This is my wand. It bonded with me . . . oh, many moons ago."

"The invitation says I needed a wand to Accept or Reject it though."

He said some unintelligible words before handing it over to me. "You can use mine. I've given it permission to perform just one spell for you."

I placed the invitation on the coffee table in front of my frozen Dad and pointed Carmine's wand at it, but I didn't make my decision just yet. It felt heavy in my hand, weightier than how a stick should feel.

"It's the magic," Carmine called to me, sticking his head in the fireplace and looking around. "A wand houses a Sorcerer's entire magic, their entire lifeblood. As Headmaster, I must admit that mine is heavier than most." He sneezed and withdrew his head, which was now covered in ash. "Your parents really ought to have this chimney cleaned."

Could I trust him? He'd already said that he didn't know Elijah, which I suspected was a lie, but I wasn't so sure. Whatever was going on, it had to have something to do with Elijah. Carmine might be able to give me the answers I needed.

I didn't have a choice.

"Wait," I said, turning to Carmine who was now looking through the downstairs closet and chuckling to himself. "The invitation says that if I Reject it, my memory will be erased and my magic will disappear. Or I could die."

Carmine shrugged as he removed one of Dad's suit jackets and fingered its material, leaning his head to the side. "Most people just lose their magic. But there's no telling what outcome will happen if you Reject. I'm proud to say that someone hasn't died in about a decade or so."

That was not reassuring. But who was I kidding? I knew I was going to Accept the invitation as soon as I'd read it. It was the only way to find out about Elijah.

I took a deep breath and pointed the end of the wand at the Accept box. A blast of gold energy emitted from it, marking the scroll. The parchment floated into the air, turned once, and then vanished.

"Good," Carmine said, putting Dad's jacket back and coming to stand by me. He placed a strong hand on my shoulder. "Well, what are you waiting for? It's time for you to start packing, sir."

Carmine took his wand from me and waved it in the air. In a *snap*, we were standing in my bedroom. "Whoa," I said, staggering forward.

Carmine waved his wand again, and my closet door burst open. My dresser did too, and my bathroom door broke off the hinges.

"Hey!" I screamed.

"Apologies," he said. "It's been a while since I have been in the land of non-magics."

I sent him a rude look as I removed my suitcases from the closet and began to load them up with things I thought I might need. Carmine took this time to settle comfortably on my bed. Between his sighs of contentment, I packed my toothbrush and toothpaste, clothes, a few coveted books, Elijah's notebook, and my phone charger.

"Is there anything I specifically need?" I asked Carmine who was now lying on my bed with his boots on.

"Nope," Carmine said, his eyes closed, a small smile playing on his lips. "If you forget anything, it will be provided for you."

"Well, I think I'm done."

"Are you sure?"

Sadness gripped me. "Wait. Can I have just one more second?"

"Take your time," Carmine said, turning over to his side.

I went to Austin's room and peeked in on him. His mouth was still open, his snoring loud and annoying. But he was still my little brother, and I would miss him wherever I was going.

I kissed his forehead. "I'm gonna miss you, little bro. But I promise, with all of my heart, that I will figure out what happened to Elijah and bring him back to us."

Mama had always told me that I shouldn't make promises that I didn't intend to keep, but I meant to keep this one. Even if my life depended on it.

"I'm ready," I said aloud when I left Austin's room.

Snap.

Carmine and I stood outside now on the porch with my suitcases. The driveway was sunken in, blasted apart by the lightning that had struck, still motionless in front of us.

"Can you please tell me when you're going to do that?" I grumbled.

Carmine ignored me and held up his huge umbrella. I grabbed my suitcases. The umbrella draped over me like a tent as we went down the steps toward a huge puddle at the head of the driveway.

"It's not raining," I pointed out. "Well, it is raining, but it's frozen in place."

"Oh, we're traveling by Puddle," Carmine said, pointing at the pool of water in front of us.

"What does that mean?"

He grinned. "It means we're going to jump inside to get to The Five Emergences. We use the waters of the non-magic world as portals to get to and from our world." His hand reached out to mine. "You might want to hold on."

"What about my family?"

"Someone from the school will visit and explain what's going on. Now, let's go to Wonder."

"Wonder?" I asked.

"It's the magical world. The world where The Five Emergences is." He peered at me and tapped my hand with his outstretched one. "Now, shall we go?"

When I grasped his hand, Carmine stepped up to the Puddle, took a deep breath, and jumped high into the sky, dragging me right along with him.

Then we slammed into the Puddle and vanished inside.

CHAPTER SEVEN

I screamed nonstop as we traveled through the Puddle, a symphony of images meeting my vision as we did. Plumes of water bubbles spread out on each side of us, each one the size of houses. As I stared closer, I noticed that the bubbles had *people* inside, all holding an umbrella like Carmine. We had entered a new world, one of flowing water and bubbles. A tornado swirled around us, pushing us forward. Nausea pooled in my stomach. Everything passed by us, including houses and birds, and I thought I even saw a huge snowcapped mountain barrel past out of nowhere.

We splashed into the ground after what seemed like an hour, and the bubble surrounding us exploded into a huge torrent of water, spreading around us like a waterfall. In fact, I realized, we were standing on smooth rock at the foot of one.

"Now you see why we need umbrellas," Carmine said, leading us out from under the waterfall as I gripped my stomach. "You'll get used to it after a while. Welcome to Wonder."

"Why couldn't we just 'appear' here with magic?" I groaned, spitting out saliva.

"Wonder is different from the human world," Carmine explained. "To enter, we must travel by different means. You'll understand as you stay here that your world's rules may not apply here. Sorcerers can travel back and forth by Puddle through every water source, but only when they come of age. You'll need an adult to give you permission to travel before then."

To gain my bearings, I looked around at Wonder and became overwhelmed immediately. We were standing on a vast stretch of sand. A huge sky stretched above us, but instead of air, it was an ocean of water, waves cresting, crashing, and rolling, their tips crusted in bright white. Occasionally, a bubble extricated itself from the ocean and fell to the ground, bursting to reveal a Sorcerer holding an umbrella. At other times, it wasn't a Sorcerer but an inanimate object that fell, like a car or a house. Somehow they didn't explode against the ground; they arrived whole and intact.

"We'll need to travel by a special Puddle to The Five Emergences," Carmine said as he began to walk over a sand dune. I followed along with him as best I could, trying not to let my fear show as a car careened down to the ground on my left side, its horn honking as it did.

"I created The Five Emergences school to train children in sorcery nine hundred years ago. I was born on the plains of West Africa, where I discovered magic and learned to channel it," Carmine began as we traveled.

We climbed over another sand dune, and an entire city appeared in front of us. But it was like no city I'd ever seen before. Purple trains zipped across the night sky, ferrying Sorcerers from one place to the next. Floating buildings rose in the distance, hazy heat emanating from them. Golden streets snaked in between the buildings that sat on the sand. All manner of creatures walked through the streets. I saw people who were dressed like Carmine, what appeared to be sentient clouds, and tall humanoid figures who had pierced elongated noses and colorful auras that surrounded their entire bodies. I even saw what looked like a werewolf shifting into human form running into a store, completely naked.

"Mr. Powers, from the time I had my Outburst, I learned to control my newfound magic on my own, fashioning the first wand from the bark of a yohimbe tree at the age of twelve."

"Were you lonely?" I asked as we stepped onto one of the golden streets. Cackling sounds came from above, and I looked up: a group of witches with green faces flew by on brooms, hurling gray clouds at one another. Wizards with long blue hats adorned with stars merged in between them, flying on air currents, disgusted looks on their faces.

"Very much so," Carmine sighed. "As I grew, I searched for other Sorcerers. My magic let me find them when they had their Outbursts. When I found them, I invited them to join me in study. Together, we learned the secrets of magic and created spells. When we realized that our magic caused us to age very slowly, we felt it was time to put our knowledge into training the next generations. So, we created the school."

Trees framed the entire city as we walked, small whisperings emanating from them that sounded like beautiful songs. When I looked closer, pretty, ghostly figures emerged from them, sparkles falling to the ground everywhere they walked.

"Dryads. You'll find in Wonder that some of us like to stay in our supernatural forms, but it is not required," Carmine whispered. I hurried to keep up, my heavy suitcases slowing me down.

"One rainy season, my new friends and I gathered, combining our magic together. We plucked a raindrop from a dark cloud, fashioning a new world from its depths. We called it our 'wonder,' and so that became its name. In it, we built The Five Emergences, and the world around it. When we had finished, we established ourselves as the first professors of the school, and then used our magic to find Sorcerer children to train. Once they graduate, some decide to live here and others return to the non-magic world."

"Wow," I said. "Have I grown up around magical people my entire life?"

"Yes. And once you go back to your world, you'll be able to see them more easily."

"How big is Wonder?" I asked, shuffling along after him.

Carmine shrugged. "Even I don't know the answer to that question. It grows as more Sorcerers move here. Because Wonder is magic, one can make it whatever they want and build whatever they want. The city we're in is where most people live and where everyone comes to first, especially new students because it provides the entrance to The Five Emergences. This city never changes. But once you go to the outskirts . . ." His voice turned ominous. "Anything goes."

At this point, we'd traveled deeper into the city. The homes were oddly shaped—some of them looked like normal houses, but others were circular, octagonal, and triangular. Some were covered in windows, and some had a misty wind drifting from them. Some were solid, some were translucent, some of them disappeared from one spot to appear in another, and others simply lifted off the ground on huge reptilian feet to settle in another place just down the road. My heart beat like a battering ram when one of the feet almost crushed me and a voice said, "Get out of the way, kid!" as the house stumbled past me.

"Keep up, Mr. Powers," Carmine said as he marched. "The homes won't hurt you . . . *much*. Plus, there is much to show you."

Carmine's expression turned dark as we rounded a corner, his index finger pointing to a golden street to our left, where a small ball of swirling black energy floated, electricity coursing around it. As I watched, the gold of the street slowly turned gray, like the magic of it had been bleached out of existence. A feeling of sadness settled on my chest, heavy and oppressive.

"What's that? And why am I feeling this way?"

The street looked like a regular street—as regular as it could look in this world—complete with large homes and perfectly manicured hedges. But farther down the street, closer to the ball of black energy, the roofs of the homes had begun to sag inward and the lawns turned from emerald to gray.

Carmine's expression turned sad now.

"The Ruin," he said. "A hungry, supernatural beast. It's been sucking the magic out of Wonder for the last year or so."

"Is somebody doing anything about"—I gulped—"the Ruin?"

He turned an intense look my way. "That's something I'll need to talk to you about. Now, follow me."

I followed Carmine to a small building that looked like a coffee shop, called The Foggy Lake. It was suspended a couple feet off the ground by smoke. Carmine muttered a word, and a cloud lifted us to the entrance. Inside it was packed with creatures of every stripe. A cyclops sat at the bar, taking up most of the space. A group of cherubs, wings extending from their backs, floated on the stage with harps in their hands, playing a soft music that almost made me weep. A gaggle of centaurs packed the back, their hooves kicking the floor, their chests bare. What looked like gnomes sat near the front, their red hats rising to the ceiling.

Carmine led me to a booth out of the earshot of everyone—or, every*thing*—in the building, and I set my suitcases on the floor before sitting down. Candles glowed in the middle, floating over the table.

"Professor Carmine, what a pleasure to see you again," a woman with white hair said, coming from the kitchen with an apron around her waist and a brown wand in her hand. She peered at me, her eyes turning from red to blue to green. "And who do we have here? Who is this cutie?" My face grew hot.

"This is Jaden Powers," Carmine said. "He's a new student at The Five Emergences. And nice to see you too, Sheila. Can you get us a cup of tea each?"

"Sure can, love. Give me just a few minutes." A commotion rang out from the back of the shop; two centaurs stood and started to push each other. "Bertram and Miren!" Sheila yelled, rushing over, lightning blasting from her wand. "I told you don't bring that crap in here!"

Sheila came back just a few minutes later with two cups, her hair tangled with leaves. After she left, two small dragons appeared out of thin air and coughed out puffs of hot smoke to heat the tea and then disappeared in flames.

"This is a lot," I said, grasping my tea and taking a sip.

"You'll get used to it," Carmine said.

Although everything was overwhelming, I was not about to forget why I came to Wonder in the first place. "Will you answer my questions now?"

Carmine took off his hat and placed it on the table. "I am at your service."

"Tell me everything you know."

Carmine snorted. "That's not a question, Mr. Powers."

I raised an eyebrow. "Tell me everything you know, please?"

"Gladly. The Five Emergences School of Magic is a school for students who show magic ability. We teach the five forms of magic: Metamorphosis, Enchantment, Elixirs, Prophecy, and the Creative Arts. You'll learn more about each type in your classes."

"Whoa," I said.

"Those are the five emergences, the categories of magic that existed in the world long before I was born. Magic I used to found my school."

A trickle of thrill reverberated through me. Would I learn how to do all of them? Man, magic would make me powerful, and no one would ever question me again.

"Wait," I said, a little disbelieving now. "When was this school founded again?"

Carmine took a sip of his tea. "Nearly a thousand years ago."

A thousand years? That's a long time ago."

He grunted. "You're telling me."

"You've been alive that long?" My eyes bugged out of my head. "Where have you been this entire time? So many bad things have happened since then. People who look like you could have used your help. Do you just protect the magical community and not the normal world?"

Carmine narrowed his eyes and was quiet for a moment before answering. "It's much more complicated than that. You're too young to ask questions such as those. You're too inexperienced to understand their answers."

I clenched my fists under the table. There it was. Again. An adult underestimating me. My parents did it all the time, and now Professor Carmine. Why wouldn't they just try explaining and see if I would understand?

"May I finish?" Carmine said, the smile returning to his face. "At The Five Emergences, children are invited when they have their Outbursts, which usually happens at the age of ten. They then attend two years later until they are seventeen."

I jumped a bit. "But . . . the car accident . . . it happened just today. I'm twelve."

Carmine grew quiet again, his eyes leaving mine for the first time, and he shifted in his seat. After a short while, he spoke. "I think I need to talk about Mr. Williams now."

I pointed an accusatory finger at him. "I knew it. Why did you lie and tell me you didn't know who Elijah was?"

He shrugged. "I felt it important to see if you would Accept our invitation before speaking about him. You needed to make this decision for yourself, not for anyone else. Plus, what if you had denied us? Your memory would have been erased anyway."

He had a point there. "Go on," I sighed.

"Elijah had his Outburst at the age of four."

"But you just—"

Carmine snapped his fingers. "Exactly. Outbursts happen at the age of ten for every Sorcerer. *Every. Single. One.* Until Elijah. When I detected his magic, I went to meet with Elijah and his parents. After studying him, I made the decision to offer Elijah a place at my school early. His parents refused my offer."

"Why would you offer at such a young age?"

"Magic that powerful had to be watched and nurtured. With no outlet, I knew it would turn destructive. I pleaded with his parents to send him to my school, but they refused. I left that night knowing that, eventually, something awful would happen, either to Elijah or to someone else."

"What happened?"

"Death." Carmine paused for a while before beginning again. "Elijah had another Outburst five years later at the age of nine, and the magic that exploded from him caused a car accident that killed a cousin of his."

"*Another one*? I thought Sorcerers can only have one Outburst?"

"By now, you should know that Elijah was different from every Sorcerer, living or dead."

My brain started to whir with information, about how everything changed when Elijah had turned nine. That was the year he went away to Hamilton and left me alone, our friendship forever changed. I gasped. "I remember Elijah's cousin dying, but I didn't know *he* caused it."

"Sadly, he did."

"He left for Hamilton after that," I whispered. "He was never the same."

Carmine nodded. "When that happened, his parents decided to take me up on my offer and send Elijah to The Five Emergences, albeit three years earlier than the required age of twelve. So, I took him and brought him here."

"Was he happy?"

A flame lit in Carmine's eyes as he remembered. "You should have seen him, Mr. Powers. You see, Elijah comes from a long magical lineage; both of his parents are Sorcerers, in fact. They lived in your world to give Elijah a normal childhood, but he was always destined to be a powerful magic worker. He excelled at *everything* at The Five Emergences, mastering every form of magic at such a fast pace that he had professors asking for his assistance. Everyone liked him, student and professor alike. Professor Nicholas Luxor, the instructor of Deterring Danger, a class that teaches students how to defend themselves, and also Elijah's favorite course, was his academic adviser."

I chuckled a bit. "That sounds like Elijah. Everyone loved him at my school too."

"I can read between the lines, Jaden." It was the first time he had used my first name. "You were the opposite from him, right?"

I ducked my head, looking into the dregs of my tea. "Yes. Always one step behind him. But I didn't mind. He was my best friend."

"Sometimes, one wants to fly though. How exhausting it must have been to always be the newborn bird."

"Wait," I said, ignoring his comment. "You say Elijah caused a car wreck? But I caused one too!"

Carmine held up both hands. "Patience. Do you want me to change tack and focus on you, or do you want to know all about Elijah first?"

"Definitely Elijah," I said, hurriedly. "His parents said that he died from drowning in a pond, but that was a lie, right?"

"Absolutely." Carmine's stare was so intense that it felt like he was looking through me, at a scene that I couldn't see. "Someone as powerful as Elijah . . . they don't just die. They *disappear*. I don't know where he could be, but I do know—"

A glass of wine flew across the room, almost connecting with my head before I ducked.

"Bertram!" Sheila yelled, running from the bar to the back of the coffee shop with her wand raised again. "That's it! You and your crew . . . OUT!"

"Maybe we should take this conversation somewhere else?" Carmine suggested. "What I have to tell you, now, is going to be very hard to hear."

I shook my head. "No. I need to know more."

Carmine took a deep breath before beginning. "The Ruin. There were rumors, Mr. Powers, *bad* rumors."

"You . . . you said it came into existence . . ."

"In the last year," Carmine finished for me. "It would appear in different areas of Wonder at first, unassuming, not danger-ous at all. I was asked to explain its origin. But I couldn't. I told everyone that since it seemed harmless, it was best to leave it alone. However, it only grew in size as time passed. And when Elijah disappeared a little more than a week ago, it started its destructive path in Wonder, devouring whatever magic it could. Wonder is slowly dying."

I gulped. "What does that have to do with Elijah?"

"I don't believe in coincidences, Mr. Powers. And no one in

Wonder does either, especially when magic is involved. You see, everyone knew Elijah was different. News traveled fast about his early Outburst, so all supernatural creatures were nervous about his entrance into Wonder. When he finally came here at nine, I tried my best to keep my eye on him. He was a fast learner, gobbling up magic like it was food."

Carmine's eyes darkened. "And he only grew more powerful as he aged."

"What are you trying to say?"

"There were rumors about Elijah from the time he came here. Even though people liked him, his fast ascent through The Five Emergences earned him several detractors. I did my best to assure people that Elijah was just a normal boy, but when the Ruin appeared, those rumors gained steam. People, including children at the school, would say that they saw him doing weird experiments with magical animals, or that they saw him flying around Wonder without a wand, or that they had seen him nestling the Ruin in his hands. Some students even reported the force of their magic was lessening over time, that even simple spells took longer to cast."

"Did you believe them?"

Carmine shook his head. "Not at first. But then Elijah came back to school early to work on a project, a week before classes officially started this year. I caught him coming out of a Puddle near the school, drenched in blood, his eyes turned blue instead of their normal brown."

"But you said—"

"That no student can use Puddles without permission,"

Carmine said, nodding. "That's when I knew that something terrible had happened. I put Elijah into an enchanted sleep and delved into his mind. What I found"—Carmine shuddered—"was my worst nightmare come to life."

He paused for a second. "Siphoning magic. The worst type a Sorcerer can use, draining the magic from others to increase their own power. We don't teach it at our school, and the knowledge of how to use it has been buried in ancient books. *That's* why the Ruin appeared. When he stole magic from others, he created a tear in the fabric of our world. And as he became more powerful, it began devouring bits and pieces of Wonder."

"But that can't be true!" I protested. "There's no way Elijah could do something that evil! He was the nicest person ever." But even I couldn't stop the doubt creeping in. The way Elijah had acted this summer was coming back to me, now—the moodiness, the sadness, the secretiveness.

"It *is* true," Carmine continued. "And I had my doubts at first too. But students had been complaining about their magic weakening for the last year. Siphoning magic makes one powerful, but its practitioner also needs to continuously take magic to keep that power. When I went into Elijah's mind, I saw him taking magic from students, magic that he had no right to."

"What happened next?" I said.

"The enchanted sleep I cast on Elijah didn't hold, of course," he said, his eyes turning stormy. "If Elijah was siphoning magic, my spell was only strengthening him. But I was too foolish to see that. The next thing I knew, he had awakened, destroyed my office, and then disappeared in a cloud of smoke."

"What? That can't be—

"I only tell you what I saw," Carmine said.

"Where is Elijah now?" I whispered.

"I don't know. The only thing I know for sure is that he was stealing magic."

"If you're the most powerful Sorcerer ever and founded The Five Emergences," I said, choosing my words carefully, "why haven't you been able to find Elijah?"

If looks could burn, I would've been ash at that moment. "Some dark magic is beyond all of our understanding."

I gripped my mug. "Well, I don't believe it. There's no way Elijah would steal magic from other people. I'm going to find him and give him a chance to explain what *really* happened."

"If you feel like you can do better than the greatest Sorcerer to ever live, be my guest," Carmine said, the joking tone returning to his voice. "Now, let's talk about *why* you had an Outburst two years after you were supposed to. Usually, Sorcerers have magic lingering in their ancestry somewhere, even if it's far back. But there's none in your family whatsoever."

"That is . . ." I wanted to say "weird," but suddenly, I had an idea. When I'd touched Elijah's papers, I had felt a sharp pain, almost like fire. Could that be part of the reason I'd gotten my magic?

"There's something unusual about you. Something strange and obscure, but powerful," Carmine said.

I decided not to tell him my thoughts just yet. I was new to this magic thing, so what if I was wrong? I had to learn more.

"If you'll allow me, I'd like to study you and your memories to try to understand where your magic came from. It can't be a coincidence that two rare magical occurrences happened in two boys who live in the same location, him having an Outburst at four and you at twelve. I think studying you could give us some answers about Elijah's own magic and help me track him down."

"If it will help you find Elijah, I'll do whatever I can to help you."

Carmine's face darkened. "Noble cause, Jaden. I will caution you though. You must not tell anyone at The Five Emergences about your late Outburst. Our magic world is one of legacy and tradition. You are a rarity, which means that the students and their families might not take too kindly to you. I'd bet word has already begun to spread even now of your entrance to our world."

"I'll keep it a secret," I said. "But why?"

"Look at your skin tone, and mine. That means nothing here, but in your world, it means a lot. People are afraid of what they don't understand. I don't want anyone to have an excuse to hurt you because of what they think about Elijah."

I let the disappointment show on my face.

"Even though I started this magical society in hopes that all would be equal here, not everyone sees Wonder the same way. There are certain magical families in this community that are wealthier than others and hold the most influence in this world. Although I was the one who categorized magic into five forms and found out how to channel those forms through a wand, making magic much more powerful than before, other creatures had their own forms of magic before I did. In Wonder, it is the fae, shape-shifters, vampires, mermaids, werewolves, griffins, dragons, banshees, wraiths, and more that hold the most power because these groups had magic first."

I shivered.

"All of these groups are proud of their original forms, though they often take a more humanlike form when at the school. I don't anticipate any harm coming to you; however, you *must* keep the age of your Outburst a secret, because I cannot protect you if they ever found out."

"I promise I will."

Carmine took a deep breath. "And there's one more thing."

"What?"

"The Ruin's continued existence is reason enough to believe that Elijah is still alive, but siphoning magic has consequences. Horrible consequences. If I don't find Elijah in time, that magic will consume him from the inside out. He will die terribly . . . and the Ruin will eventually destroy not only my world, but yours too."

CHAPTER EIGHT

After Professor Carmine's terrible proclamation, neither of us felt like finishing our tea. We left The Foggy Lake, and Carmine used what he called a Cloud enchantment to fly us on fluffy, cold clouds to Matthias's Wandshop for the Bondless at the top of a snowcapped mountain. The store was nothing more than a small cabin with smoke drifting from a chimney. I followed Carmine inside, shivering the entire way. An older white woman stepped out of the shadows into the main room, wearing a flowing red cape.

"Elsia Matthias!" Carmine called lovingly, giving her a strong hug as I sat my suitcases down. "I have a new student for you."

"Professor Carmine," Elsia murmured, allowing him to kiss her cheek. "You know I don't like stragglers. But I'll give you this favor since you are Carmine of all people."

"Thank you," he said, bowing to her before turning to me. "This is Jaden Powers."

"Oh, I know who you are," she said, grasping my hand in a vise grip. "How are you, Jaden?"

"I'm fine," I said. "I need . . . a wand?"

"That you do," she said, letting go of my hand and taking hers out of her pocket in a flourish. She muttered a spell. The entire room went dark. When it lightened again, the room was filled with floating wands of all colors and lengths.

"Whoa," I said as I looked around. It was like we had been transported to an entirely different building; the entrance to the shop had disappeared, and the inside of the cabin suddenly looked so big I could barely see the walls. When I walked forward, the wands all swirled around me, shining and glinting, like they were urging me to take them. I reached out my hand.

"Careful," Elsia called. I turned to see her and Carmine standing what looked like two football fields away. I hadn't realized I had walked that far. "A wand has to *bond* with you."

"How do I find the right one?" I called back.

"I can't answer that. Pick the one that seems to call to you. Everyone is different."

Everywhere I moved, the wands followed me, shifting from side to side, floating in the air. Electric energy shot from their tips, brushing every part of me. I half expected them to hurt, but all I felt was . . . *love*, to be honest. An intense love that felt like my parents. A deep place in my heart stung at the thought of what they must be going through now that I had left home.

I thought about Austin and his constant snoring, and I hoped that he was doing all right without me. He had already lost Elijah, and now I was gone too.

A comforting wind blew around me as I contemplated the floating wands, as if they heard my thoughts. I closed my eyes, hoping to see if any wand would somehow call to me. When I opened them, a familiar feeling of hopelessness filled me. What if I couldn't bond with a wand? I'd had my Outburst late; what if I couldn't actually do magic? And even if I could, what if I wasn't any good at it? I wasn't very good at normal school. Wouldn't I be even worse at a magical school?

Sweat beaded on my forehead as I pushed both hands in my pockets, shuffling from foot to foot. I looked away from the wands, my lack of confidence returning with an intensity that I hadn't felt in a while.

When I felt this way, Elijah was always the one to reassure me. He would tell me that I was good enough, that I meant something to people.

As I thought about Elijah, an ivory-colored wand floated right in front of me, its light pulsating brighter than the others. Maybe it was meant to be mine.

When I reached out to it, an invisible air current picked me up from the floor, pushing me into midair so I could reach the wand. A warm sensation traveled through my body as I grasped it. Was this what it meant to bond with a wand?

Then a sharp buzzing filled my body, like a swarm of angry bees. Suddenly flame shot out of the end of the wand, and an invisible force blasted me across the room, smashing me head-first into the opposite wall.

I awakened to find Carmine and Elsia standing over me.

"What happened?" I moaned.

"Rejection," Elsia said. "The wand you chose refused the bond."

"Can I try again?" I said, my heart beating rapidly as I stood. I didn't want to be a failure here. What would happen if I couldn't bond with a wand? Would they send me home and erase my memories?

Elsia shook her head. "No. Unfortunately, the wand you picked is the only wand that can bond with you. It rejected you, so there's nothing else we can do." She nodded to Carmine. "Thank you for bringing him, but he must leave now." She waved her wand, and the lights dimmed for a moment, then brightened again, and Carmine and I found ourselves standing in the cold snow outside the warm shop.

CHAPTER NINE

Tears welled in my eyes as we stood at the edge of the mountain near Matthias's Wandshop.

"I can't even get one thing right!" I picked up a rock and threw it off the mountain, only for a translucent spirit that looked like a young boy to catch it and throw it back at me, cackling as he flew away. Who knew what would happen to me, now? I wasn't good at anything, and now I'd blown my one chance to find Elijah.

"I'm probably the first kid in the history of Wonder that's about to be kicked out before even stepping foot at The Five Emergences," I groaned.

A comforting hand squeezed my shoulder. "All is not lost."

"What do you mean?" I said, wiping my eyes.

"I think it's time we travel to The Five Emergences," Carmine said, whipping out his wand.

"But I don't have a wand," I whined. "I can't do magic without it."

"Would it have been great if a wand bonded with you the first time you tried? Sure. But there is something called the Bond Trials that students participate in when they can't bond with a wand the regular way. Would you like to participate?"

My spirits lifted. "I'll do anything for a wand."

"I must warn you; the Bond Trials can be very emotionally taxing."

I gulped. But if this would help me find Elijah, I had to do it. "I still want to do it."

"Wonderful! Are you ready to travel to The Five Emergences?"

I nodded. "Yes!"

Carmine paced around me, tapping his chin with his fingers. "Hmm, you're a Sorcerer, so you have to look the part, and you need your classroom materials. We don't have time for shopping, so I'll just conjure some for you. The words I will use for this spell are kpọọkuo ihe omụmụ ụlọ akwụkwọ. Repeat the words after me."

"Kpọọkuo ihe omụmụ ụlọ akwụkwọ," I said.

"Good." Carmine tapped both of my shoulders with his wand and said the words. Wind kicked up on the mountaintop, sending snow blasting and swirling across the clearing. A portal appeared right next to me. Packages flew through it and floated around me. Carmine flicked his wand, and one of the packages opened. Clothing zoomed out of it. A snow-white cloak fastened itself to both of my shoulders with buttons

75

cascading down the front. It was asymmetrical, with the left side flowing past my knees and the right stopping at my stomach, and a hood attached. The pants were black, made of material that I'd never felt before, fitting against my legs like a second skin as they magically replaced my suit pants. My new shirt was made of that same material. Instead of tennis shoes, boots attached to my feet, stretching up my legs, buttons replacing the laces. A red bow tie appeared next, replacing my tie.

"Whoa," I said as my clothing changed.

"You look like a real Sorcerer, now," Carmine said.

Multiple suitcases appeared out of the portal too, landing at my feet.

"You'll need extra changes of clothes," Carmine pointed out.

"Is that it?" I said. I swirled around in a circle, then checked my appearance with my phone's camera.

"You'll need school materials too," Carmine said, pointing his wand at the portal.

Books and crystal vials poured out of the portal. A backpack appeared next—an all-red one to match my bow tie. "Chekwaba akụrụngwa," Carmine said, pointing at it and making me repeat after him. "This spell will protect and hold all of the materials and equipment you're bringing with you."

I looked at everything he had given me, plus my own suitcases from home. "*Everything?*"

"Yes, everything," Carmine said. "And it'll only respond to your voice. Here, put your backpack on the ground and open it." I did as I was told, and, when prompted, picked up my suitcases from home and the new suitcases with my new materials. They all got lighter and smaller as I aimed them toward the open backpack and pushed them inside. After I closed it, I put the backpack on my back; it was surprisingly light.

"I think I'm gonna like this world," I mused, laughing.

Carmine laughed with me. "It'll only get better once you get your wand. *Now* it's time to go to The Five Emergences." Carmine swept his wand across the clearing and said another spell. "Gbanwee nkume." Rocks lifted from the ground and shook violently in the air. I remembered the ghost throwing a rock at me and prepared to duck.

"The first spells were enchantments. This spell is metamorphosis, changing an object's physical properties." The rocks above me exploded in a bright light, causing me to close my eyes. When I opened them, two winged beasts the color of a blue ocean stood in front of me. Their lower bodies looked like horses, but that was pretty much the only similarity they had. Golden wings attached to their backs, sweeping the air in complicated arcs, sending showers of dust to the ground. Their faces were angular, and their mouths snorted fire. Spikes rose all over their body, except for their backs.

"What are these?" I marveled.

"Haizum," Carmine said, jumping on one of them. "Not the real ones though. I transformed the rocks, which means the spell won't last long. Hop on, Mr. Powers. And don't worry about the spikes; they are only used for defense."

Nausea roiled in my stomach. "Why can't we take a Puddle? I'm a little scared of heights."

"Oh, we will. Like I said before, we have to take a special one. Hop on, Mr. Powers."

When I did, Carmine pointed his wand into the distance. "Off to The Five Emergences we go."

We shot off into the blue sky, my stomach rolling over and over. I clasped my hands around the haizum's reins, forcing my gaze to the creature's blue fur. The wind was deafening. I closed my eyes and hoped that the trip would be over soon.

Jaden, you'll only get to experience this once. The thought startled me. I didn't normally think of myself as brave. But I was *flying*. Was I really going to spend the whole trip with my eyes closed?

I opened my eyes and immediately regretted it. The haizum dipped low, falling toward the bottom of the mountain, and then in a fast *swoop*, it swept upward, wind blasting my clothes until I almost lost the reins.

I screamed as my haizum followed Carmine's higher and higher. We crested low-hanging clouds, which drenched me in water, and then dipped back downward. I kept screaming until I had no voice left. We soared below a vast ocean sky, waves crashing and thrashing. That scared me, but seeing a huge outline of a black whale coursing through the waves scared me more. It opened its mouth and swallowed a huge amount of water, and I felt myself being pulled in with the force. A blast of light flew past my head, a barrier forming around me.

"Mr. Powers, keep up!" Carmine yelled from his haizum,

his wand pointed at me. He flew into the distance, and I followed.

"How am I supposed to keep up? As if I know how to fly this cursed thing," I muttered through my teeth, holding the reins so tight that I thought my fingers would break.

I followed Carmine toward a strangely misty part of the ocean sky. He flew into it and suddenly disappeared.

"Oh no, oh no, oh no," I screamed as I went after him.

We flew into the mist. Cold wrapped around me until I shivered. I couldn't see anything but gray—not even the haizum underneath my body. After a few seconds, the coolness lifted, and we emerged into a warm, blue, cloudless sky. The haizum dipped low and settled on green grass, Carmine dropping right in front of me.

"Welcome," he said, "to The Five Emergences."

The mist cleared, and the school came into view. It was an enormous palace, spread across five mountain peaks. Five obsidian towers rose into the air, so large that I got an "ant" feeling from them, their tips cresting the clouds. Golden words were etched into their centers, naming the five types of magic that Carmine had listed earlier. These towers were connected by a building made of big, heavy, silvery stone. Well-kept gardens with fragrant flowers, gorgeous trees, and trimmed bushes decorated its outside. A large wooden door protected by multiple elaborate stone arches was positioned in the building's middle, with an actual drawbridge in front, leading over a moat filled with sparkling pink water.

Carmine pointed at the palace with his wand, and the five

towers shifted, their tips morphing into something else. "Metamorphosis," he said, gesturing to the one on the far left. The top of it was now a large butterfly with rainbow-colored wings, but when I blinked, it changed to a humongous egg, a crawling green bug that turned in circles, and then changed back to a butterfly. He motioned to the tower next to it. "The tower for Enchantment is one of my favorites. As you can see, the moat's water is pink, but its color changes from time to time." Sparkles of light swirled around the second tower, its tip stretching into the sky like a princess's enchanted prison, fireworks booming in the air above it. He signaled to the tower in the middle, which was now a stoppered bottle of boiling liquid. I squeaked when a large spider the size of a building crawled over it. "Elixirs. For those students who dare brave the brewed arts." He waved at the fourth tower, which had turned into a gigantic swirling ball that revolved in a circle, repeatedly. "Prophecy." Finally, he moved to the last tower, where a large firebird jumped from the sky and breathed fire from its throat, screeching the entire time, so loud that I had to cover my ears. "Ahh, the Creative Arts. This emergence will test your mettle and courage, I should say."

Another haizum dropped out of the sky at that moment, falling next to mine as Carmine strolled forward. A white boy sat on its back, about the same age as me. Brown curly hair framed his head, and curious blue eyes peered at me. His cloak was black, and so was his bow tie. Unlike me, a wild grin spread across his pink lips.

"Jeez, that was fun!" he yelled.

"Speak for yourself," I grumbled, jumping off my haizum.

The boy followed behind me, sticking out his hand. "I'm Mikael Levine, a first-year. You?"

"Jaden Powers," I said. "A first-year too. Why are you alone?" I pointed at Carmine who was feeding his haizum something from his wand.

Mikael gasped. "You came here with *the Headmaster*?"

I shrugged. "I guess. Am I supposed to be impressed?" I didn't mean to be rude; I really didn't know if I should be or not.

"Heck yeah! Carmine is the most celebrated Sorcerer of all time. If it weren't for him, we wouldn't even be here."

"Well, that's who I came with. How are you here without an escort?"

Mikael jumped up and down once. "It's because I know all about the school already. I live in the normal world, but my parents are Sorcerers. The Five Emergences has a program where Sorcerer kids who live in the human world get to visit the school before we start. It's supposed to help us get acclimated to the magical world. So, I've traveled here a lot over the years. I know my way around already."

"Ooh, that's cool," I said. "I'm from the normal world too. But I think that I'm gonna need as much help as possible."

Mikael nodded eagerly. "I'll help you! I know almost everything about The Five Emergences, and I even know a few spells." His face fell as he averted his eyes from mine. "Not that that will do anything for me. I haven't bonded with a wand yet."

81

"I don't have a wand either," I said. Mikael's eyes lit up.

"Good," Carmine said, walking over to us. "I'm glad that you've met each other. I knew Mr. Levine would be coming, and I have already arranged for you to room together. Mr. Levine, please answer any questions Jaden has and help him while he's here."

Mikael grew quiet, staring at Carmine in awe.

"Mr. Levine?"

"Su-sure, I'll help him." Mikael gulped. "I've just been here so many times, and I've never seen you, sir. You're amazing."

When Carmine chuckled, his cloak rose around him, flying in nonexistent wind. "The Bond Trials will commence first thing tomorrow morning. I think it's time for both of you to get some rest."

"But I'm not tired," I complained. "I'm more excited than anything else."

Carmine grabbed both our hands and walked us across the moat, the haizum disappearing in gold sparkles. "Oh, I think you will now feel the passage of time."

As soon as Carmine said it, I did. As we crossed the moat, the sky darkened immediately to the point of blackness. My body grew heavy too, as I realized it must have been hours and hours since Elijah's memorial. I checked my phone. The clock on my cell cycled through numbers so fast that I couldn't keep up.

"It'll need to be recalibrated to Wonderian time," Mikael explained as Carmine tapped his wand on the door. It opened at his prompting. "You'll need a wand for that though."

"It is time for bed," Carmine said again as we went inside, turning to us in the interior of an enormous hall. Black marble spread on the floor as far as the eye could see, and seven staircases rose in the distance. "Every student is now asleep, and the first day of classes is tomorrow. It's time for you to rest for the Bond Trials." He winked at Mikael. "I assume you know where the dormitories are?"

"Ye-yes, sir," Mikael managed to say.

"Good," Carmine said. "I'll see you first thing in the morning, before the rest of the students awaken."

He then disappeared in a shower of blue light, leaving Mikael and me alone.

CHAPTER TEN

We stood alone in the hall after Carmine vanished, my yawns stopping me from being in full awe of my surroundings. I stared around at the seven staircases. Mist hovered over them, flowing from their bottoms to their tops.

"Which one should we take?" I asked.

"Follow me," Mikael said, walking toward the center one, which was the color of the deepest night. "The center staircase always leads the first-years to their rooms. There are more in the palace that lead to the subject areas."

"What do you mean, 'subject areas'?" I said, following Mikael up the winding staircase.

"Do you know the five forms of magic?" Mikael asked.

I took another step. "Yeah, Carmine explained them to me."

"Each student gains a specialty area in their second year,"

Mikael said. "You'll pick one with your academic adviser at the end of this year."

"Oh, okay, I guess," I said as I huffed along. "How long do we have until we reach our rooms?"

I made the mistake of looking back. Even though it seemed like we had been climbing for at least ten minutes, I could still see the door we had just come through. Eerie.

"Welcome, first-years," a disembodied voice said as Mikael jumped onto a stone platform. I followed behind him. The platform rose until we came to a long hallway. The walls were bare and made of concrete, but the floor was made of the same black marble as below.

"Hey, Aibell," Mikael said quickly.

"Who's that?" I whispered.

"Well, crap," the voice said. A woman appeared out of thin air, wearing a gray veil over her sunken face, and a green, ripped dress. As she rose a few inches off the floor, gray feet with black painted toenails stuck out of the hem. "I thought I'd scare you, but I guess you're smarter than that." She did scare me, and I jumped a bit, but calmed down because Mikael didn't seem fearful at all.

"That's Aibell," he said. "She's a banshee. She's in charge of the first-year dorms. Not sure how she ended up here though. She's not scary, don't worry."

Aibell rose to her full height—which wasn't that tall—and ascended higher in the air, a hazy heat emanating from her body. "Oh, how dare you! I'll have you know I'm the scariest of the banshees." And with that she began to wail, screaming so loudly that I was sure that any sleeping students were going to wake up. My eyes widened as her mouth elongated and black sludge fell out of it to the marble, disappearing in hot steam when it made contact.

"Aibell, stop," Mikael commanded, and she did. "Can you just take us to our rooms?"

The banshee sighed and then turned around and floated ahead of us. "Follow me," she grumbled.

"What the—" I mouthed to Mikael, who just shrugged.

We walked down the hallway a ways. Then Aibell took a wand from the folds of her dress, tapped it against a wall, said a hurried spell, and then disappeared. A beautiful cherrywood door appeared in the concrete, our last names etched into it. "I guess we're officially roommates," I said.

"Good," Mikael said, opening the door.

Inside were two large beds, both already made up with heavy-looking white blankets and soft pillows. One lone window spread in between them, a small lamp on the windowsill providing the only light. Two other doors were inside, one leading to a bathroom and the other a closet.

I removed my backpack as Mikael took out his wallet.

"Is that enchanted?" I asked, pointing at it.

"Sure is." Mikael smiled. "Mom charmed it before I left."

I placed my enchanted backpack on the wooden floor, pulling out the suitcases filled with my books, school materials, and clothes. Mikael's belongings plopped out of his wallet. He ran his mouth a mile a minute as I put things in our shared closet and bathroom.

Mikael pointed at one of my books, *The Five Emergences, A History of Sorcery*, which I was placing on the small bookshelf by the bed I chose on the left.

"Carmine wrote that one," he said. His name was written across the spine in black letters.

I took out another book, *The Common Dreambook, Spell-casting for First-Years* by Nazine Ashmore. My curiosity got the best of me; I sat on the floor and tried to open it, but it was glued shut by some force. "We don't have a wand yet," Mikael pointed out. "It's also against the rules to look at the spells until after our first class."

"So much information!"

"I know, right?" Mikael said, words spilling from his mouth like a raging waterfall. "I'm just so excited to finally be here. I mean, I've already been here a million times, you know? And read all about it, you know? But I'm finally a *student*! I mean—"

"A million times, huh?" I said, cutting him off. "So you know a lot about this school?"

Mikael nodded energetically, his hair bouncing up and down in such a rapid motion that I was sure he was giving himself a headache. "Yeah, like I said, my parents are Sorcerers. In fact, everybody in my extended family is too. Most of them live in Wonder, but my parents moved to the human world when I was born. Over the years, though, they made sure I knew enough about The Five Emergences before officially coming here."

Doubt weighed heavy on my shoulders. "You must not be nervous," I whispered. "I'm very nervous. I don't know anything about magic."

Mikael's face drooped. "Like I said, I don't have a wand either. I'm the first one in my family not to bond with one on the first try. I see the looks my family gives me, and hear my parents whispering when they think I'm not listening. They worry about me, and I worry about myself here too. I want a wand, but I'm afraid that I won't be able to bond with one, and then Professor Carmine will send me home."

I nodded. "It's good to have someone here who's going through the same thing I'm going through. I just want to be successful here, and I think I'm already starting off on the wrong foot."

Mikael sat and scooted closer to me, placing a hand on my shoulder. "I get the fear, but don't worry too much about it. Every student in our year starts off the same way—we are all here to learn and grow in our magic."

"Speaking of students," I said. "I'm actually looking for one. His name was Elijah Williams, and he was from the normal world too, and—"

Mikael's eyes widened as he stood. "You—you know Elijah Williams? *The* Elijah Williams?"

"I mean, yeah, he's my best friend. Do you know him?"

"Who doesn't!?" Mikael picked up his wallet and whipped

out a humongous poster, which he then proceeded to hang on the wall with thumbtacks. And there he was, Elijah looking outward with that familiar smirk, that smile that he used when he knew something everyone else didn't. A long wand that looked more like a scepter rested in both of his hands, and a black cape was fastened to his shoulders, floating around him in an oval shape. A golden luminescence surrounded his entire body, and light burst out from his wand.

"Whoa," I said again. "That's him. That's Elijah."

"*Everyone* knows Elijah Williams," Mikael said, smiling a proud smile. "The greatest kid Sorcerer ever to exist. That's your friend for real?"

"Yep, that's him." It was comforting to see that not only I admired Elijah, but everyone else did too. At first. He was always impressing people, and it seemed like it was no different in the magical world . . . until it turned on him. My face fell.

"Man, Elijah was *everything* to the magical world," Mikael said, excitement filtering through his voice. "You see how huge his wand is? That's because he excelled in every type of magic, to the point where he was helping professors teach their classes, and he would also help with problems in Wonder. He was so popular that even the Sorcerers in the normal world knew about him." Mikael sighed. "Man, I wanted to be him so bad."

"Do you know what happened to him?"

Mikael's voice lowered. "No one knows. People . . . they loved him at first, but that all changed when the Ruin appeared, and the rumors started about him siphoning magic. After he disappeared, Carmine announced that everything was true and that Elijah was behind it all."

"I don't believe Elijah would do something like that."

"To be honest, I don't either. My parents tell me all the time that the first story told about a villain is probably not the correct one. Elijah did too much good here to be some evil Sorcerer."

"For real?"

"I mean . . ." He pulled out another poster from his wallet. It was a picture of Elijah standing outside a body of water, his wand in hand, a scary monster towering above him with multiple tentacles. "He defeated the kraken! Well, *one* of them. It was threatening a whole town. They say it almost killed him, but he blasted it into little pieces, and kept a piece for himself as a souvenir. No adult Sorcerer had been able to take one on, but Elijah was able to. That's why I don't think he caused the Ruin or that he was siphoning magic."

"Whoa, he did all that?" It wasn't too surprising, but, wow, Elijah was having all these adventures while I was stuck in public school. And he was keeping so much from me. I felt like I didn't know him anymore.

"Yeah," Mikael said as he pinned the poster on the wall above his bed. "He is amazing." Mikael sighed as he sat on his mattress. "They even say that his magic rivaled Carmine's. I'm not sure how true that is, but, dang, I wish I could've met him." Admiring eyes turned to me. "But you knew him. Well, *know* him. Wow, who would've thought that I would be rooming with Elijah Williams's best friend?"

"You . . . you don't hate him, then? I know most people do."

Mikael shrugged. "I'm from the normal world. My parents knew enough not to believe the first negative story *anyone* told about a Black boy. I choose to believe that he was and still is a hero until proven otherwise. Maybe the siphoning magic part is true, but there's gotta be a reason why he needed to use that type of magic. There's no way he could've been stealing magic from the school and its students for himself. I mean, come *on*, he rescued a town from one of the kraken for Wonder's sakes!"

We sat there for at least the next hour, talking about Elijah. I told him all about how he was in the normal world, how he was the bestest friend ever, and how I came to the magical world to find him.

"You didn't come to learn magic?"

"It's a good side effect, I guess," I said, shrugging. "But I really wanna find out what happened to him. His parents deserve to know. *I* deserve to know." I paused.

"Will you help me?" I asked. "I'll need someone who knows everything about magic."

"Yes, I'll help! But we need to be careful; most people hate Elijah." Another look of awe traced his face. "Wow, I get to find out what happened to Elijah Williams. Who would've thought?"

He pulled his pajamas from his wallet, put them on, and crawled into bed. "We should sleep; Carmine is going to be here tomorrow morning for the Bond Trials." And with that, Mikael rolled onto his side and was knocked out almost immediately.

I took a shower and changed into my pajamas, uncertainty and inadequacy settling on my shoulders. Mikael knew all about Elijah and his magic, and he didn't even know him personally like I did. Elijah had told me nothing. Of course, I knew he had been sworn to secrecy, but I was his best friend!

The bed was comforting, and Elijah's poster on the opposite wall was a welcome distraction for my mind. For years, I was living next to a Sorcerer and didn't know it. I wished he had let me in on his secrets before . . . everything else happened. I only hoped that I could leave a mark on the world like he had. But how could I? What if I wasn't good enough to save him? I didn't even have a wand!

Mikael's soft snores helped me nod off to sleep, and the last thing I saw was Elijah's poster and the large wand settled in his hands.

CHAPTER ELEVEN

Aibell's wailing woke me up the next morning. Mikael moaned and put his pillow over his face.

"Aibell, shut up!"

"I'm just dropping off something!" she yelled back, thrusting two envelopes under our door. Her wails dissipated as she floated away.

"Is she like a supernatural alarm clock?" I grumbled.

"An alarm clock and babysitter," Mikael groaned.

I picked up the first envelope. Inside was a letter from Carmine with simple instructions:

Take the center stairwell upward to my office—HSC

I called out the instruction to Mikael who simply nodded and went into the bathroom.

The second letter was from Mama and Daddy, their address stuck to the outside of the envelope. My heart squeezed when I thought about my family; Carmine had said someone would reach out to them about me. The squeeze turned to a rapid beating as I read the letter:

Dear Jaden,

We are so proud of you. And we miss you already.

We feel that you should've at least told us you were leaving! But, someone from the school has explained everything to us, and we understand that we couldn't make the choice for you. While we think that we should have had a say in you going to this "magic school," we know now that that's not how it works there. Please do the best you can and be safe; we hope to see you soon whenever you get a break.

We love you.

The tears burned my eyes. I turned around when Mikael came from the bathroom, looking out of the window so he wouldn't see me cry. The night was just changing to morning, blueness peeking out of the blackness, no sun or cloud in the sky.

"You okay?" he asked.

I nodded, wiped my eyes, and then we hurriedly dressed and left the room. We stumbled past a wailing Aibell and went to the staircase, but it stopped at the first-year hallway.

"Um?" Mikael said.

"Any ideas?" I asked.

"No. Carmine's office was never on the tours."

The top of the staircase glowed red when both of our feet stepped on it.

A male voice spoke. "Permission granted to Professor Carmine's office."

The top of the staircase removed itself from the structure and rose in the air as one platform. "Whoa," I said, grabbing on to Mikael's hand tightly. The platform flew across the palace, past the seven staircases. As we climbed higher, I could just make out students of varying ages spilling out from their hallways, heading to their respective stairwells.

The platform climbed higher once more and then stopped outside a hallway.

The male voice spoke again. "You have arrived. Have a great day."

"That really sucked," I said, holding on to my stomach.

A bright red door was the only thing in the hallway, and it opened as soon as we drew closer. Inside, Carmine sat behind a large desk, writing something on parchment with a feathered pen. Another student stood in front of him, a sour look on his white face. His face was angular, and so were his ears; the upper part of them stretched upward in a slanted line. Arrogant and annoyed purple eyes glanced over us, his mouth turning downward in a frown. His neat emerald hair looked as if he didn't allow a single strand to be out of place. But it was his aura that really made him different; a purplish glow surrounded his entire body, and it seemed as if a peppermint scent radiated from it, filling the entire office space.

Carmine picked up his wand when we arrived and stood behind his desk.

"Mikael and Jaden, meet Silas Rivers, first-year student, and fae prince of the Summerlands."

I reached out a hand. "Hello." That only intensified Silas's sour look.

"*Silas*," Carmine said.

Silas sighed and grabbed mine with soft hands. His grip grew stronger as he squeezed. He did the same for Mikael.

"It is time for the Bond Trials," Carmine announced, pointing his wand in our direction. "Its purpose is simple, to bond with a wand. Coming here is an extraordinary step, but now you must face your real challenge." He didn't even give us a chance to ask questions. "Shall we begin?"

I opened my mouth to speak, but Silas interrupted me. "Yes, Professor."

Carmine uttered a spell. "Malite ule nkekọ."

The office dissolved, like someone had taken the surroundings and shaken them with all their might. I spiraled in darkness, dark smoke rising around me. My boots settled on a hard surface, the smoke an ever-present feature of this place.

"Jaden?" Mikael coughed. I breathed a sigh of relief. At least Mikael was here with me.

"I'm here."

A dark, crumbling mansion rose in front of us, a night sky

96

stretching above it. In a swirl of smoke, Silas appeared next to me, his aura providing the only light.

"Where are we?" I asked.

"The Bond Trials, obviously," Silas said. The arrogance in his stare had traveled to his speech.

"We should probably stick together," Mikael said as we looked at the mansion. "I don't know what type of magic this is."

Silas scoffed, his sour gaze falling on us, his frown becoming even more pronounced. "Fools at The Five Emergences? What a shame."

"We're not fools!" I responded.

Silas sucked his teeth. "Whatever. Look, there's a powerful wand in there, and it's *mine*. My parents pulled strings for me to get into the Bond Trials, so you'd better stay out of my way when we're inside. Got it?"

And with that, before we could even respond, he strolled inside the mansion, slamming the door behind him.

Mikael stiffened. "Don't worry about him. What he says doesn't matter."

"*He's* the fool."

Mikael groaned. "You don't understand. Silas is the heir to the Summerlands, the fae kingdom outside of Wonder. He's from a very powerful lineage; they had magic before Carmine, some thousands of years ago." He shivered. "Silas might look human, now, but that's not his original form."

"Carmine did say that supernaturals can shape-shift."

Mikael smiled a bit. "Yep. It's so cool to see, but the fae can still be scary though."

"He's not so better than us, considering he don't have a wand either."

Mikael shrugged. "I don't know. You're from the normal world too, so I'm sure you understand how people *pretend* to be better than others based on some superficial reason."

"Good point."

A blinding light brought my attention back to the task at hand. A light the color of gold suddenly emanated from the left side of my chest. It moved every time I breathed, jumping up and down.

"What's this?"

Mikael pointed at his own light. "Our soul."

"As if *that's* not creepy," I muttered.

"It's anchored with magic back to Carmine's office. We need to go inside and get our wand."

"I—I don't want to."

Mikael grabbed my hand, and we walked forward. "We can go in together."

But as soon as we closed the mansion door behind us, I found myself alone in a large, black cavern.

"Mikael?" I called. No response. I walked forward once, my feet crunching over hard dirt, and then stopped. Deep fear settled inside me, causing me to shiver. My heart beat so loudly that I thought it would fall out of my chest. I rested a trembling hand over the glowing orb. *I can't do this. I just can't do this. I need to go home.*

But that would mean I left Elijah wherever he was. And if he could survive this world for years, so could I.

My eyes adjusted to the darkness as I stepped forward. Thick stalactites glistened on the top of the cavern, the ends of them stretching toward the ground. I must've traveled from inside the mansion to underneath the ground somehow.

A light radiated from the distance, which guided me along a dark path. It led me to a clearing of sorts, where three large openings bored into the rock. Three wands hung in the air, floating above my head near the entrance of the openings. Soft breezes emanated from them, brushing against the dust on the ground. Just like they did at the wandshop, they called to me in ways that I couldn't quite understand. I admired them all, a metal one in the middle, a black one whose color reminded me of Elijah's on the left, and a blue one on the right.

"How do I pick?" I whispered.

If Mikael was here, I could ask him, but he wasn't. As I took the time to think, more wands appeared in the space, shining immense light on the surroundings. I looked around me; carvings were etched into the walls. I ran my hands along them, gasping as I realized what I was seeing. A large tree rose from the ground, dry grass surrounding it. A young boy appeared as my hands traced the carvings, his face the color of night. A wand sat in his hands as he stretched it toward the tree. It was Carmine, gaining his wand from the yohimbe tree. I felt an emotion, but it wasn't mine; it was love, filtering through me as Carmine performed his magic.

I knew what I had to do now. It wasn't that I needed to pick whichever wand I wanted—it was that I needed to pick one that reminded me of love. That reminded me of Elijah. And the black one reminded me of the one I'd seen on Mikael's poster. I went to the opening and reached out to the wand, but it moved deeper inside the cavern, its light guiding the way.

"Come on." I gritted my teeth as I followed it. Every time I reached for it, it skittered forward, sometimes crashing into the walls. By the time I caught it, I was dripping sweat, and I stumbled to the ground in another clearing.

The wand vibrated in my hand as a harmless flame licked up from its bottom all the way to its tip. I felt at peace as I regarded it, feeling deep in my soul that it was mine.

A deep voice sounded in my mind. "Do you accept?"

"Yes," I whispered.

The wand moved of its own accord to the middle of the rocky clearing, lifted upward, and then blasted out smoke. Ghostly images emerged from its tip, screams piercing my eardrums as they did. There were so many of them that I couldn't tell what I was supposed to be looking at.

I heard Dad's voice first. "Go to your room, Jaden!" The image grew until translucent figures appeared, Dad in his work suit and me sitting on the couch in our living room facing him.

"But I don't want to," the ghostly Jaden argued.

"You do what I tell you to do," Dad said. I remembered this night. It was after my grades fell when Elijah left for Hamilton for the first time. I had been out of control, not knowing until later that it was grief. Dad continued to argue with me, until the scene flipped back to the beginning, us arguing once more.

The next image exploded from the wand, the last basketball game between Elijah and me where we had argued, right before his parents said he had died. Tears stung my eyes and fell as the scene looped over and over of us fighting, of me getting on my bicycle and riding away from him.

The wand pointed at me now with a mind of its own, and I lifted into the air, screaming. Another image of smoke emitted from its tip, revolving around me like a tornado. It was the car crash, the Outburst that I'd had. *No, no, no, I don't wanna see that.* But I was forced to watch as my feet crashed into the ground. It was the largest image of them all, of Austin asleep and me opening my eyes, blasting the car to pieces as it careened to the side of the road. When the flames licked the air, the image looped and re-looped, playing over and over again.

"No," I said, dropping to my knees, clutching my head. "I don't want it. I don't want a wand. Take it away from me."

When it settled in my hand, I threw it across the cavern, but didn't hear it clatter.

Go to your room, Jaden!

Just admit it. You'd rather be at your fancy school than with me, wouldn't you?

I hope Jaden is okay with everything that's going on.

The words repeated themselves, a cacophony of sounds that clanged in my ears like a discordant record.

"All that you have been fighting for has led to this," a voice said. My chin lifted. "Do you not want your wand?" The images muted, but the pictures still moved, a horrible reminder of my past.

"Stand."

My legs moved and forced me to stand. A figure stepped from the gloom, a pure white, tall figure with no face, almost like a solid ghost. I wanted to recoil from this . . . *thing* . . . that stood in front of me, to close my eyes, but it was like something held me in place.

"What makes you think you even deserve a wand?" The figure spoke, but not aloud—the words reverberated in my head like a stereo drum. I couldn't see its face, but it almost seemed like it was sneering at me as the images floated around it.

"Why are you here?"

The figure raised a white hand, and my wand flew toward it.

"Answer me!"

"I want to find my friend," I whimpered.

"*Coward,*" the figure said. "Pure cowardice."

"I'm not a coward."

"You're either a coward or you're not *good* enough to be here."

My fists clenched. "I *am* good enough. I know I am." My stomach lurched as I lunged forward at the figure to wrestle the wand from it. It swiped the wand through the air, and an unknown force pushed me aside like I weighed nothing. Then the figure pointed toward the image of me and Elijah.

Horror gripped me as I realized what was happening, stopping me in my tracks. The Elijah in the image closed its eyes and lifted out of the picture, coming to rest right in front of me. He smiled at me before ropes appeared out of thin air, ropes that wrapped around his face and pulled him backward toward the figure. Elijah began to scream bloodcurdling screams as they wrapped around his nose, his chest, and his legs.

"Elijah!" I screamed, holding out a hand, too scared to move.

The figure continued to point the wand at Elijah, the ropes squeezing tighter and tighter. "Is this who you came for?"

I had to get my wand. It was the only way that I could get Elijah back, to save him. The force of my will made me move again, my boots running across the cavern. The figure swiped again, and this time, flame erupted from the wand, lashing out at me like a whip. I dodged it and continued to run, but not before Elijah screamed once more, falling to the ground as the ropes covered his mouth.

"No, Elijah!" I screamed, jumping toward him. I crouched and did my best to remove the ropes that bound him. Choking sounds emitted from his throat. "You're not going to die!"

The figure spoke from opposite me. "But that's what he's meant to do. You can't save him. You're not good or strong enough." Wait. That voice was familiar.

Wind kicked up, and the rocks underneath my feet rolled away. *Whoosh.* The wind blasted me, picking me up and throwing me across the space, pinning me against the cavern's hard rock. Blood spurted from my mouth as I groaned. The figure dropped to all fours, stalking me now. I emptied my mind and let all fear drop away as it jumped across the gravel and fell in front of me, a mouth and jagged teeth appearing on its once blank face. It roared so loudly that my clothes rippled. Still, I did not allow the fear to take control of me.

Elijah gagged from where he lay, his chest heaving slower and slower.

"You're not meant to save him. Let him go. This is his fate."

There it was again, that familiarity. I *knew* that voice.

"You don't deserve to be here. Go home."

That voice was *me*. My inner voice telling me that I wasn't good enough. That Elijah was better than me at everything. That I couldn't save him.

I wouldn't allow that voice to tell me that I shouldn't be here.

My right hand rose of its own accord. The wand in the figure's hand flew out of it and into mine. The fire whipping around the room branched back to the tip of my wand, and then I slashed it around the cavern, directing it at the figure. It exploded in showers of light, disappearing into nothingness, taking the floating images with it.

Elijah remained, the ropes dissolving. I approached him with the wand in my hand. He gave me a slight smile.

"I will find you," I whispered.

He nodded once, and then he too disappeared.

I stood in the cavern, breathing hard, my wand fastened to my hand. The completeness felt *right*.

I had bonded with my wand.

And I would do my best to be the best.

CHAPTER TWELVE

We found ourselves back in Carmine's office, each of us holding a wand. "Great work," he said.

Mikael dabbed at his eyes, while I wiped blood from my
chin. Silas stood near us, but his demeanor felt as if he were
miles away. Annoyance flitted through his eyes.

"That . . . that was *not* what I thought it'd be," I said.

Carmine laughed a bit. "Bonding is hard work, even for
ones who don't have to go through the trials. But the wand is
yours now. May I see it?"

I shook my head. "No."

Carmine clapped his hands. "Good! *Never* give another
Sorcerer your wand, unless you really mean to." His eyes wid-
ened, and his smile disappeared as he looked closer at the wand
I was holding. "Wait. That wand . . ."

"It reminded me of Elijah's," I said. "The one from the poster Mikael showed me."

Silas turned to me now, pointing, recognition in his eyes, his aura turning a dark shade of red. "That's the bristlecone wand!"

Carmine stood tall, taking a deep breath. "I don't think you realize which wand you have captured, Mr. Powers."

Mikael gasped. "Jaden, that wand hasn't been bonded with since . . ."

"Since I fashioned it a thousand years ago," Carmine finished.

"Wait, this wand used to be yours?" I asked, turning wide eyes to Carmine.

He shook his head. "No, I created it from the bristlecone, the oldest tree in the world, thinking that its age would create the most powerful wand. But I had already bonded with my wand years before. It refused me, so I let it"—Carmine waved his fingers—"drift off into the ether. I wasn't sure anyone could ever . . . How in the world . . . ?"

"That's not fair!" Silas bellowed, stepping toward me and Mikael. I pushed Mikael behind me, holding my wand tightly. "That wand was supposed to be mine!"

I raised my wand to him, unsure of even how to use it. "Well, it chose me. Step back."

"Jaden, no!" Mikael said.

"Stop, now." We looked at Carmine, whose eyes had turned steely. "Silas, a wand chooses its owner."

"But it should be mine!" Silas growled.

"By whose order?"

Silas grumbled, but didn't respond.

Carmine pulled out sheets of paper and handed them to us. "These are your schedules. Go clean yourselves and go to class. You now have your wands. Use them wisely and learn deeply." He turned his attention to Silas. "And *you*. You and your parents would do well to remember that although you're royalty in the fae world, The Five Emergences is *my* world."

Silas growled again and huffed out of the room. Carmine sighed, sitting back in his chair. "Go to class."

Mikael and I made our way to Carmine's office door.

"And, Mr. Powers," Carmine called to me. "Don't forget that I'll need to study you later."

"Yes, sir," I said, stepping out of the room with Mikael.

After taking a quick shower, changing our uniforms, and picking up our backpacks from our rooms, we went to the first class on our schedules, Magical Theory.

"What happened during your trial?" I whispered to Mikael as we walked down the first-year staircase to the main floor of the palace, students of all different species streaming past us.

"Dead bodies," Mikael said, shivering. "I had to search for my wand through all these piles. I almost ran away multiple times. You?"

"Images," I explained. "As soon as I touched the wand, all of these images exploded in the cavern I was transported to, all horrible scenes from my life."

"You would think it would be easier to get one of these darned things," Mikael grumbled as a hairy mountain troll pushed me out of the way, shifting into human shape as it did.

"But why was Silas acting like that?" I said, straightening my clothes. I sent a glare the troll's way.

Mikael led me down a hallway and then found a nook where we could speak alone. "We have about five minutes until class starts. The bristlecone wand is one of legend, and people have wanted it for centuries. They have even tried to manipulate their way into the Bond Trials to get it. Everyone who has tried has failed. You're the first person it's ever chosen. Silas is a prince—he probably thinks he's entitled to that wand." Mikael was eyeing the coat pocket where I had stashed it. "His parents probably told him his entire life it belonged to him. But like Carmine said, a wand chooses its owner, so of course it wouldn't bond with people like Silas or his family. Wands don't like to be manipulated."

"Is he *that* entitled?"

Mikael shrugged.

A scream pierced through the crowd of students, like an alarm sound of some sort.

"We'll need to talk later," Mikael said, dragging me out of the nook and heading to an opening in the wall on the left. "Class is about to start."

We entered. The classroom was filled with a mixture of

students. Most of them were human, like me and Mikael, while others were in different phases of shifting from the supernatural. As Mikael led me to two seats in the back, I walked past a Black girl with gills on her neck and long braids, a Latino boy who spontaneously burst into flames every so often, another boy with sharp pointed teeth and red eyes who was nursing a cup of red liquid, and a white girl whose hair seemed to be writhing with snakes—but when I blinked, it turned back to normal.

I rummaged through my backpack as I sat down, pulling out *A Theory of Sorcery & Spellcasting*, and waited for the professor to appear. The room darkened and then *bang*! A Black woman materialized at the front of the room, the sound of birds singing heralding her entrance.

"I'm Professor Amadi Hadiza," she said dreamily, holding her wand aloft. "As you'll notice, the first-years are split into two groups this year." That explained Silas's absence.

Mikael whispered to me. "You should take out your notepad; she tends to drone on and on."

That was fine with me, especially since I needed a break from everything I'd gone through the last few days. When I looked at my textbook, I noticed that she was the author. I pulled out my notepad and a pen as Hadiza spoke a spell, directing her wand at the board. "Dee." A piece of chalk floated upward, writing on the board as Hadiza spoke.

"Turn to page five in your textbooks to keep up with me," she began. "However, I have found that writing down notes helps with retaining information."

She paused for a moment before beginning. "You might have noticed by now that your dreambooks are locked. They will be so until this class has completed for the day. Before you can practice magic, you must know what magic is and where it comes from." She walked up and down the aisles as she spoke, her braids sweeping through the air. "You must know how it works, how it is used, how spells are cast, and how they are created." Multiple chalks of various colors flew into the air, drawing on the board pictures of a vast universe, complete with planets and stars. "Magic is a form of energy, one of the fundamental aspects of reality and, as far as I can theorize, as old as the universe itself. To my knowledge, it burst the universe into existence, leaving remnants of itself throughout the cosmos."

The chalk drew pictures of an exploding star across the board, and then creatures appeared, human and supernatural alike. "It seeped into all space, creating galaxies, stars, and planets. Remnants of it fell from stars and onto planets, burying within their crusts and then into their earth. As humans evolved, it interacted with life-forms on Earth for the first time, either by manipulation or—as I theorize—of its own volition, creating magical creatures first and then Sorcerers."

A drawing of Carmine appeared next with a wand in his hand, five blasts of energy emitting from it. "Carmine was the first human to have an Outburst of magic as far as we can tell, and he was the first to manipulate it. He also recognized that it seemed to manifest itself in humans as they turned ten, but it's not known *why* yet. As Carmine grew older, he sought out other magic users, who became the other founders of The Five Emergences." Hadiza smiled.

She paused at the front of the room and just waited. The silence deepened until someone raised their hand. It was the Black girl with the gills on the side of her neck, her skin glowing with an emerald undertone.

"The supernaturals came first, right?"

"Your name?"

"Scion. Scion Midra. Water nymph of the kingdom of Atlantis."

Atlantis? That's actually a thing?

"Yes, Scion, the supernaturals came first. For thousands of years, they lived with magic without human interference."

"In fact, water nymphs were the first supernaturals to build our cities with magic," Scion said, her voice taking on a tone of pride. "We didn't use wands in those times. Our cities glimmer with gold and rubies, and our songs have caused the waters to expand. We rule the seas for a reason." Her face darkened. "That is, until the fae tried to take our lands for their own. But we fought them off and won."

"That is true," Hadiza said. "The supernaturals need no wands to do magic; wands just allow a user to channel the magic inside of them into one point, helping to intensify their mental concentration on the outcome of the chosen spell. Humans aren't innately magic. If they don't bond with a wand, their magic eventually destroys them. We aren't yet sure why magic chose humans after centuries of only bonding with supernaturals, but we know that it did."

A Black human boy raised his hand. "Justice Cameron, here. Does that mean that magic has a mind of its own?"

Hadiza snapped her fingers. "*Exactly.* It can and does act on its own at times. Although Carmine was a mastermind to manipulate it, it doesn't mean that magic won't evolve once again."

"What does that mean?" Justice asked.

"It means that while for now fashioning wands makes magic easier to channel, it doesn't mean that it will *stay* that way. As a theorist, I can only hope that magic has reached its final stage of development, but I may be wrong. I want to be right, but who knows?"

Mikael raised his hand now. "Mikael Levine. It's been a thousand years since the first wand was created though."

"It has, which makes me think there is no more development that magic needs to take currently."

A flurry of questions continued for the next hour, and I did my best to capture everything on my notepad. All of this was fascinating to me.

I was so absorbed with my notes that when Hadiza asked for any last questions before the scream sounded, I made the mistake of raising my hand with my wand outstretched.

Hadiza gasped. "You have the bristlecone wand?"

Crap. "I—I guess."

Hadiza strolled to the front of the room as every wide eye turned to me. "What is your name?"

"Jaden Powers," I said.

"Hmm," Hadiza said, placing her hand underneath her chin. "I don't know that last name, so you're not a heritage student. You must be from the human world?"

"I am," I said, stuffing my wand back into my pocket. "My best friend used to go here. Elijah Williams."

Everyone in the class gasped, whispering among one another. Scion's face turned bright, and one of the snakes in the girl's hair from earlier fell to the floor. Hadiza froze for a second, the color drawing from her face. "What is your question?"

Crap to the second power. I mean, I was *going* to ask her a question about Elijah, but I wasn't going to mention his name. Too late now.

"Professor Carmine told me that Elijah had his Outburst at four, and that's why he came here early. Is there a reason magic acted differently for him?"

Hadiza smiled. "I can only talk about what I *think* happened. Most of my theories have proven true, but I don't have any about Elijah. All I know is that he was a prodigy and that he was well suited to achieve here. Before . . . the Ruin."

My question poured out before I could stop it. "Do you think the Ruin appeared because Elijah was siphoning magic? I know that's what most people believe."

Hadiza's smile disappeared, and she cleared her throat before speaking. "When a Sorcerer siphons magic from another, the action creates a rip in reality, a gash in the universe. That rip eventually becomes a Ruin, sucking up all the magic in its wake until everything is extinguished. The Ruin appeared when Elijah was accused of siphoning magic from our students at this school. So, yes, I do believe he was the culprit, and why the Ruin exists."

The class began to mumble now, continuing to speak among themselves while sending me curious looks.

Justice Cameron glared at me. "Of course he'd ask a question like that," he whispered.

The boy who kept catching on fire rolled his eyes. "Everyone knows Elijah was the cause of the Ruin. He's the reason why the supernatural world is being eaten away." The girl with snakes for hair nodded in agreement, tossing him a tense smile.

"I probably shouldn't have said anything," I whispered to Mikael.

"You must all understand that the Ruin is the greatest threat we've ever faced, and it's the first time in our history that we've had to deal with something like this. Siphoning magic is so mysterious that we don't know much about it." Hadiza pulled a book from her desk, swiped her wand over it, and drawings lifted into the air, circling one another. A swirling ball of energy came into view. "As you can see, the author of this text only theorized that something like that could happen, which is why these are just drawings. But, taking magic from others is the worst thing you could do, taking away what makes them who they are, taking away a piece of their soul. This creates rips in the fabric of what's natural and creates the unnatural. The Ruin is unnatural, and it will eat everything in its wake if we don't find a way to stop it."

She turned fearful eyes to us as she finished her statement. "If we don't find a way to stop Elijah."

You could hear a pin drop in the silence that followed.

"Class is over," Hadiza announced as the chalk wrote homework instructions on the board, as if she hadn't just said the worst thing possible. "You will read chapters two and three in your textbooks, on spell creation. We will talk about why spells are created and the steps you can take to create new ones for next class."

As students streamed out of the classroom, I looked at my schedule to see which class was next. It was empty.

"Oh, we have Advisement next," Scion said, coming to stand in front of me and Mikael. She was tall and absolutely beautiful, like she could be a model. Her hair flowed down her back in long braids, and she wore what looked like an emerald toga with a flowing cape of the same color around her shoulders. The sound of tinkling harps met her entrance, and a scent of oranges infiltrated my nose every time she moved.

She shifted uncomfortably. "Don't mind that. That's just how I am."

"You're literally a water goddess," Mikael said.

When Scion laughed, it was like the room was shaking. "I'm not a goddess. People just think we are because of the stories that have been told about us." She reached out a hand to me, and when I grasped it, warmth spread through my entire body, and I smelled sea salt. "For what it's worth, I don't believe that Elijah was siphoning magic, or that he's the reason why the Ruin exists."

I breathed a sigh of relief. "Thank you."

"We should all be friends," she continued, nodding at Mikael. "I'll see you soon." And with that, she walked out of the room alone.

"Did she just tell me that we are now friends instead of asking?" I asked.

Mikael placed his backpack on his shoulders and stood. "She's a *goddess*, Jaden. You don't just say no to her. Come on, let's get to Advisement."

Words bloomed on my schedule now. "It says that I have to meet with my academic adviser, Professor Cinxia Menifee," I said. "There's nothing else after that. I'm not sure where her office is."

"Oh, she's the new Deterring Danger professor," Mikael said as we walked out of the classroom and into the crowded hallway. He pointed to concrete stairs that led downward. "She's in the basement."

"Wait. That's the class that Carmine said Elijah loved the most! Maybe I can start looking for him by getting some answers from her?"

Mikael shrugged. "I don't know, maybe. I mean, she's new, so she might not know much. Professor Nicholas Luxor was the professor of that course before she was. He retired unexpectedly when Carmine told the world about Elijah."

"Why?" I asked.

"Well, it's all speculation, but Elijah was his assistant when he was at the school. He was the smartest kid here, so Luxor took him under his wings to teach him magic. We think that Luxor felt guilty about how Elijah turned out, so he left teaching in shame."

"That's . . . interesting."

"I'll meet you back here when you finish with Menifee, and we can go to our next class together?"

"Sure," I said, hoisting my pack over my shoulders. "See you soon."

CHAPTER THIRTEEN

I knocked on Professor Menifee's office, the only one I could see in the basement after walking down the concrete steps.

The door opened, and a blond woman stood before me, wearing sunglasses—I wasn't sure why she wore them in a damp basement—and a workout jumpsuit.

"Mr. Powers?" she asked, looking down at her hands as she shuffled papers.

"Y-yes?" I responded.

"Come in," she said, gesturing toward her desk, which had two chairs set in front of it. I took a seat and marveled at the bookshelves lining every corner of her room; the biggest one behind her desk held a large slash in the wood near the top. I gasped at the sight.

"Oh, that?" she said, pointing at it as she sat down. "A feral werewolf gnawed at it while it was trying to kill me." She spread out her arms. "As you can see, I'm still here, and it's not, so . . ."

I said nothing. I mean, what could I say?

She placed her papers on the desk. "So, I see I'm your academic adviser. I've heard a lot about you, Mr. Powers."

"Already?" I said between tight teeth.

She tipped her sunglasses to her nose and stared down at me with intense blue eyes. "I do my best to research all my first-year advisees for the school year. I know you come from the normal world."

I remembered that Carmine had told me not to tell anyone about my Outburst; however, he never said I couldn't talk about Elijah. Heck, she'd find out anyway from some other student if I didn't tell her.

"My best friend was Elijah Williams," I blurted out.

Menifee sat back in her seat, surprise blanketing her expression as she took off her sunglasses. "Mr. Williams, hmm? That's something I don't hear every day. I saw that you were from the same city as him, but I wouldn't have dreamed you knew him personally."

"I did," I said. "And I want to know everything that happened to him. Carmine told me some things, but I want to know more."

She narrowed her eyes. "You think you can do more for Elijah than Carmine is doing? That you can find him when Carmine couldn't?"

"More *for* him?" I asked.

"If you've spoken with Carmine, then surely you know what happened to Elijah?"

"The siphoning magic," I said. "He . . . he implied that Elijah had turned evil. I don't believe that."

Menifee shrugged. "Dark magic, Mr. Powers, tends to do just that. I wasn't the Deterring Danger professor last year, but I did work with Luxor occasionally. I saw Mr. Williams . . . change. He was once jovial and happy all the time. But then he grew moody, distracted, distant, and he started disappearing for days at a time. Finally, I stopped him once and asked what he was doing, and he said that he was working on some secret project. I mean, Mr. Williams was *always* working on something or another, some new spell, some new illusion, but this was different. He seemed like he was changing in ways that I didn't understand, and still don't. After that, students started complaining about their magic being weakened, and of course, parents blamed the child that they used to think was a hero."

"Elijah," I breathed.

She nodded. "Everyone knew he had his Outburst early. After that, Elijah disappeared completely, I got Luxor's job, and the Ruin grew more, wreaking havoc all over Wonder. It even devoured parts of the palace before Carmine banished it and put protective charms over the school. Who knows how long they'll last though?"

"Do you believe Elijah was behind all of it?"

"Yes," Menifee sighed, the strength in her expression and the toughness of her body weakening like a deflated balloon. "He's the only one that had the magical strength. I mean, professors would too, but none of us are quite as strong as Elijah. Also, siphon magic isn't common knowledge. No professor here knows how to use it."

"You think a kid would know about magic that adults don't know?" I said, rolling my eyes. "I'm unconvinced." A thought popped into my head though, something I hadn't realized until now. "My friend Mikael *and* you just said that Luxor left."

"Luxor resigned, yes."

"Maybe it was him that's behind it all? Maybe he was using some other magic to . . . I don't know . . . I don't know nothin' about magic, I—"

Menifee's eyebrows arched. "Let me give you some advice, Mr. Powers," she said. "Deterring Danger is all about questioning the way things appear to be. But right now, you need to learn as much as you can." She took the closed slip of paper from my hands and spread it open on her desk. When she tapped it with her wand, a bright flash bloomed before my eyes. "The rest of your schedule should appear here when it's ready. We didn't get to talk about your time here, but I think I have an idea of what you want to do."

"You're telling me I need to let Elijah go?"

She shook her head and handed me my schedule. "I'm telling you that you need to *learn* magic in addition to snooping around." She inclined her head toward me. "You may leave now."

What? I didn't know what I was expecting, but I knew I wasn't expecting *that*. I needed to know more. "But—"

"You *should* take a look around and try to figure this mystery out," she said, winking at me. "I have a feeling that you're not going to stop until you get answers, and I like that. Just make sure that you study too. Now, go to class."

She turned her back from me and shuffled the books on the bookshelf behind her, ignoring me completely.

❧

"Um . . . where is our next class, Enchantment, again?" I said, looking at my schedule as I stumbled back to the hallway where Mikael was waiting for me.

A box marked *Enchantment* had appeared on the paper, but the schedule didn't say where it was, only a small poem:

NO ONE EVER ACCUSED US OF KNOWING
HOW TO WRITE POETRY

Magic doesn't have to be mundane or boring
It can inspire, affect, alter, enhance, and endow
Learn how to create and inspire
A whirlwind awaits you—you just need
To have the courage to take it for a ride.

I groaned. "It doesn't even rhyme!"

Mikael checked his as we streamed into the hallway with the rest of the crowd.

"I'm not sure where Enchantment is."

I raised an eyebrow. "Didn't you come here for tours?"

"I mean, I did, but I didn't know that we'd have to solve riddles to—"

Silas stepped out of the crowd around us, surrounded by two boys and one girl, pointing his wand directly at me. "Dapu n'ala."

An unseen force grabbed me by the ankles, and I tripped over the floor, my backpack falling to the ground and all my supplies falling out. Silas and his new friends laughed as they passed by us.

"I bet you're just like Elijah," he spat.

The rest of the students milling in the hall started to laugh too. I even heard someone say, "Probably just as evil."

"Are you okay?" Mikael said, helping me to my feet. I started stashing my things back in my bag.

"I guess word has already spread," I grumbled.

"Looks like it," Mikael said.

"Well, my wand is *mine*, now. He needs to get over it. Him and his friends. We need to hurry and find our next class."

Mikael read the poem again. "I just need to remember," he whispered to himself. His eyes widened after a while. "I know where it is! It's not really *in* the palace."

"What does that mean?"

"I mean, it's in the palace, but it's not really a physical classroom." He pointed at the word "whirlwind." "It's an enchantment, and how much you wanna bet it's inside of a whirlwind?"

"Where in the world do we find a whirlwind?"

Whoosh. Students screamed as they jumped out of the way of a swirling gray cyclone barreling down the hallway, sending papers and books flying everywhere. Mikael grasped his wand. "Come on," he said as we dodged it. "We need to catch it!"

We ran down the hallway in its direction. Someone screamed behind us, "Are you kidding? That's a cyclone! You're going to die!"

"Wait, what if we die?" I said, huffing and puffing as my chest began to ache from the run.

"It's just an enchantment," Mikael said as the cyclone burst through the entrance of the palace. "While they can and do hurt sometimes, their effects don't last."

We followed a stream of first-years outside and watched as they slipped inside the tornado, turning over and over again, yelling along the way.

I tensed. "I don't know if we should."

"Scared?" someone said from behind us. It was Scion, standing tall and proud. "I wasn't sure which enchantment would be used today."

"Today?" I said. "You mean it changes every day?"

Scion shrugged. "That's what I heard." And with that, she ran to the tornado and jumped in.

I gulped. "I don't know about this."

Mikael grabbed my hand. "Let's just do it. If you die, at least I'll die with you."

"That doesn't inspire confidence," I muttered. But it couldn't be that bad. Right?

We ran at the same time, and before we could even jump, the tornado caught us in its winds and lifted us upward. Our hands disconnected as we screamed. I felt like my body was being torn apart as we swirled in the dark grayness. Tendrils of wind whirled around us as we tumbled and bumbled like we were in a drying machine. I was gonna kill Mikael if we got out of this alive.

With a *bump* I crashed into the seat of a desk, pain ratcheting through my tailbone. "Whoa!" With a scream, Mikael fell from the top of the tornado. Although his face collided with his desk, he merely bounced unharmed to the floor.

"Are you okay?" I said, holding out a hand to him.

"It didn't hurt," he said, his eyes dazed as he sat in his seat.

"They could've kept that tossing and turning though. Ugh."

Other students began to fall into the classroom until every desk was filled. Scion moved her desk across the room to sit beside me and Mikael when everyone else conveniently scooted away. Although it looked like we were inside a classroom, the walls were nonexistent, just tendrils of wind whipping back and forth.

A male professor burst through the cyclone, drifting on dark clouds, thunder and lightning blasting from inside them.

"Whoa," everyone said at the same time.

"Good morning," the professor began. "I am Professor Siberius Cayman. Welcome to Enchantment." He floated around the room, his white cape fastened to his shoulders. His blue eyes were so bright that I had a feeling he had enchanted those too. "Enchantment spells are charms that affect reality," he began, flying to the top of the cyclone. "Everything you see around you is an illusion, a charm. Enchantments last as long as the person casting them can hold them. The stronger the Sorcerer, the stronger the enchantment."

Cayman swept down in front of us again, brandishing his wand. The pencil I held floated in the air and then turned into a golden bird, singing a beautiful song. After a while, my pencil returned to its normal state and settled on my desk.

"Enchantment is *not* metamorphosis," Cayman warned. "Enchantment changes the appearance, it enhances, and it is not permanent. While metamorphosis changes one living thing to another, different living thing. In enchantment, if you require beauty, you can attain it. If you require ugliness, that can be attained as well. Enchantments are one of the most used forms of spells Sorcerers use."

Justice Cameron raised his hand. "Can we learn that flying enchantment?"

The clouds settled Cayman on the ground. "It's not a flying enchantment because I'm not actually flying. The cloud is. It's the one you'll be learning today, the Cloud enchantment. Open your dreambooks." I grabbed mine from my backpack and turned to the page Cayman indicated and read the spell.

"Urukpuru ga efe efe," Cayman said. "Follow along with me."

We repeated the words.

"Now, say the words aloud," Cayman instructed. "And you'll be able to fly! Stand up." With a sweep of his wand, our desks disappeared, leaving open space. "Take a partner and start practicing. After that, we will work on another enchantment."

Mikael grabbed me, and we went to the side of the room as students partnered with one another.

"Okay," I said nervously, looking down at my dreambook once more. "This is the first time I'm performing a spell." Although I was anxious, pure excitement buzzed in me.

"Oh, this is gonna be fun," Mikael said. "Urukpuru ga efe efe." Rain clouds burst from his wand and settled near his feet. "Oh jeez, oh jeez, oh jeez," he said, taking a hesitating step forward.

"Go for it!" I encouraged.

Mikael took a deep breath and jumped on the clouds. They lifted him up in the sky a few feet before fear drowned his eyes. In a huff, the clouds burst, and he fell on the floor, splattered with water. "Ugh," he said, wiping at his eyes and his now soaked hair.

I flipped through my dreambook and found a drying enchantment. I wasn't sure if we were supposed to be doing any other spell besides the Cloud enchantment, but it was as good a time as any to practice more. "Kpoo ntutu isi a," I said. A blast of hot air exploded from the tip of my wand, and Mikael careened across the room. Everyone in the class laughed, including Peter, the boy who seemed to be made of fire. He stopped laughing when the warm air dissipated his fire—he looked just like a normal boy, now.

"Ah, ah, ah," Cayman said, flying over to us on his rain cloud. "That's the wrong spell, Mr. . . ."

"Jaden Powers," I said.

"Mr. Powers. A drying spell can't be used to counteract enchantments," he said as Mikael made his way back with a scowl on his face. "You'll need to dissipate the magic by banishing it. That spell is . . ." He swiped his wand Mikael's way. "Ịchụsa." Mikael dried completely, his uniform returning to normal. "You're not drying the spell; you're acting like it never existed in the first place." He winked at me before speaking to the entire class. "I probably should've told you that from the beginning, but I wanted to see how you handled it. Good try, Mr. Powers."

Mikael grumbled under his breath as Professor Cayman strolled away.

"Wanna keep trying?" I said as the flaming student flew past us screaming, his fire returned.

"Peter Garcia, no flaming in the classroom!" Cayman said, flying past us as well. "Why must seraphims be so annoying?"

"I guess." Mikael shrugged. "But it's your turn."

I took a deep breath. I'd already chosen the wrong charm to help Mikael. What if I performed this one wrong too? Maybe the bristlecone wand was too powerful for me? Maybe it had made a mistake in choosing me? I'd already had my Outburst too late; what if I wasn't cut out to do spells? Sweat beaded on my forehead as I concentrated on my lack of self-confidence. Mikael patted my shoulder as I looked away from him.

"Hey, you can do this," he said with a smile.

I nodded and directed my wand at my feet. "Urukpuru ga efe efe." Clouds formed under my feet for a second, but then disappeared. I repeated it, and clouds came again, but this time,

128

they towered over my head before sputtering out. Cayman was like a constant sentry, sweeping above me on his cloud to give me more pointers.

"Mr. Powers, enchantments—well, *all* spells—are about mental fortitude, or the *intention* one puts behind casting them. You aren't even gripping your wand tightly; it hangs loose from your wrist. Grip it tighter, clear your mind, and use your intention. Finally, keep your mind strong to stop the clouds from disforming. You've already proven you can do spells when you used the wrong charm for Mikael. Use that determination to guide you."

I gripped my wand as he flew away. Scion floated above us now, smiling a little bit. "It's easy," she bragged before thundering away.

"Don't listen to her," Mikael said. "Just do what Cayman said."

Spells are all about determination, I thought as I gripped my wand tighter. *I want to fly. I want to fly. I want to fly.* I said the spell aloud and pointed at my feet once again. Rain clouds formed, dark and black, a quiet thundering sound booming. I stepped on the clouds and felt they were solid to the touch, even though they shouldn't have been. They lifted upward almost immediately.

"Whoa," I said as I careened higher.

"Use your wand!" Cayman called to me. "Direct your path."

I pointed downward, floating back to Mikael at eye level. I smiled. "I did it! It's your turn!"

Mikael grinned and took another deep breath. Clouds

formed and lifted him too. This time he kept his balance and used his wand to direct himself near me.

I directed upward where students were beginning to fly across the classroom, some of them nearing the eye of the cyclone.

"Should we?" I asked.

"We should," Mikael said eagerly. By waving our wands, we flew all over the classroom, yelling as we did. I bumped into Peter, who flamed out before bolting ahead of me. After a few minutes, Cayman towered over us all.

"Are we ready to go?"

"Go where?" Scion asked.

He pointed to the eye. "Outside, of course."

Nervousness flitted through my stomach as everyone else whooped in excitement. With a flourish, Cayman disappeared out of the cyclone, and the rest of the class followed. We flew above the ramparts and towers of the palace, then dipped low to the now purple water in the moat. Someone's cloud burst and they fell inside, but Cayman did a quick spell and righted the situation almost immediately. They sputtered as the cloud re-formed underneath them, and we kept going while I laughed.

We climbed higher into the air now, soaring over the entire palace, my breath catching at the sight. Birds of various shapes, sizes, and species soared around us. One made of fire flew past me, almost bursting my cloud. One had three heads, screeching through all its mouths as it careened through the blue sunless sky. When we dipped closer to the ground, a huge, tentacled creature rose from the water's depths.

My fear got the best of me; my cloud burst, and I fell screaming toward the moat. I cleared my mind and set my intention. "Urukpuru ga efe efe!" I screamed. The cloud re-formed, picking me up just as a tentacle reached out to grab me.

The tornado roared near me, appearing out of nowhere, and I followed Cayman and the rest of the class back inside. Peter crashed into one of the desks, Justice and Scion gracefully fell to their feet, and Mikael and I steered ourselves to their side. Everyone else came into the tornado in various positions, huffing and puffing along the way.

Cayman stood in front of us, his eyes wild. "Good job." He sent an intense stare Peter's way. "For *most* of us." He glanced at me. "And, Mr. Powers, the way you saved yourself before I could shows a mental fortitude that I haven't seen in previous first-years. Looks like being from the normal world has no bearing on your performance here."

Enraged looks bore down on me from all directions, except from Scion and Mikael. I even heard someone say, "It's because he's a siphoner like Elijah."

"Now for the second part of the lesson," Cayman began, pacing in front of his desk.

I almost died, and there's a second part of the lesson?

"Enchantments can also be used to augment." That was the only thing he said before he pointed at Mikael. "Gbanwee uwe a." Roses appeared on Mikael's cape, drowning it from top to bottom. Mikael yelped. A lovely aroma passed by my nose. "This is a general spell, but you can use it to change your clothing any way you'd like, as long as you keep your mental anchor

131

strong." With a swipe of Cayman's wand, Mikael's cape returned to normal.

"Seems easy, doesn't it? It's not as easy as the cloud spell, because changing one's appearance requires a fortitude that some of you may not have yet. Now, let's practice. The first partner group that gets it right *and* sustains the enchantment will retain a minute head start on the final at the end of the school year."

The snake-haired girl raised her hand and introduced herself as Gorgona. "What is the final?"

Cayman winked. "Wouldn't you like to know?"

We spread out again, practicing the enchantment. Cayman was right; it was a hard spell to master. After fifteen minutes, I had managed to change Mikael's boots to green, but I was only able to hold it for three seconds before they returned to black.

"Gbanwee uwe a," Mikael said, sweat pouring down his face. My bow tie turned from red to purple, vanished in thin air, and then my shirt caught fire.

"Hey!" I yelled. Cayman swept in front of me, dispelling the magic.

"Careful, Mr. Levine," he groaned, strolling away to help other groups.

"Can we take a break?" Mikael asked. "You can't cast any spell if you're tired."

"Good point," I said. Mikael and I stood by Cayman's desk, watching everyone else struggle too. As Scion pointed her wand at Gorgona and the snakes in her hair turned to pool noodles, I noticed a framed picture on Cayman's desk.

"Hey!" I whispered to Mikael. "Look at this."

My heart clenched as I recognized Elijah, standing next to someone I didn't know. The man had dark hair and wore a button-down shirt, with a red cape drifting over his shoulders. They both held wands. "This is Elijah. Who's that?"

"That's Professor Luxor," Mikael whispered back. "The old Deterring Danger teacher."

"You and Menifee told me that Luxor resigned after Elijah disappeared," I said. "That seems a little fishy. Do you think that Cayman knows something?"

Mikael shrugged. "It wouldn't hurt to ask."

After I succeeded in turning Mikael's hair pink, and after he turned my pants yellow—which, to Mikael's delight, refused to turn back—I went up to Cayman as he watched the class. I approached cautiously, unsure of how to bring up the prominently displayed photo.

"Um . . . Professor Cayman?"

Blue eyes peered at me. "Mr. Powers, how can I help you?"

"I—I noticed that you have a picture here of my best friend, Elijah Williams, along with an old professor. D-did you know Elijah?"

Cayman's forehead furrowed. "What are you talking about?"

I pointed at the photo. "That's Elijah Williams and Professor Luxor, right?"

"Is this some type of joke?"

"No, I'm not—"

"Yes, I knew Mr. Williams. Who didn't? He was a prodigy, a great Sorcerer and would've probably been *the* greatest Sorcerer in the future. But this photo, my boy, does *not* have Mr. Williams in it."

He was right. The only person present was Luxor, a slight smile on his face, standing in the entrance of the palace.

"Wait, I know I saw—"

Cayman sneered. "You *saw*? The enchantments must be getting to your head, Mr. Powers. You shouldn't speak on things you don't know. Luxor and I were great friends, and he was a powerful Sorcerer. But I have no clue what happened to Mr. Williams."

My face burned as he addressed me. He might as well have been my parents giving me a lecture. But one thing was clear: Cayman had become defensive. Which meant he was probably hiding something.

Cayman clapped his hands for everyone to hear. "Class is now over. Go through the spells in your dreambook and try to do some enchantments on your own. Mr. Powers and Mr. Levine sustained their enchantments first, so they have earned the credit on the final exam. And remember, intention is key. I'll see you next time."

He waved his hand, said a spell, and he, his classroom, and the tornado disappeared, leaving us outside the palace's unlocked doors.

CHAPTER FOURTEEN

Silas and his three friends stopped us in our tracks as soon as we staggered into the palace to head to the cafeteria for lunch.

"Hello," Silas sneered at me and Mikael. "Did you enjoy Enchantment? We're heading there now."

Most of the class, including Justice, Gorgona, and Peter, sidestepped us and kept moving down the hallway, leaving Mikael and me alone.

I gripped my wand, but I hadn't learned any spells yet to protect myself.

"Leave us alone," I said, staring deep into his eyes. Although I had a guess that as a fae, he'd been learning magic for years, I refused to let him think he could intimidate me or my new friend.

One of Silas's friends, an Arab girl, snickered, placing both hands on her face. "'Leave us alone,'" she mocked.

"Nahri, don't scare them just yet," Silas laughed. "And, Erick and Sean, be nice."

"So, you were friends with Elijah Williams?" a white boy who I assumed to be Erick asked, leaning closer to me.

"Yeah," I said, trying to stand up taller. "What of it?"

"Did he ever do magic around you?" Sean, a Black boy, asked.

"No, he didn't," I said. Then I remembered our basketball game before he disappeared and the way he whispered to himself sometimes, but they didn't need to know that. "Why does that matter?"

Silas snickered. "Rumors. People said he was always whispering to himself in the corridors of the palace, creating spells."

"They say there hasn't been a student who's ever been like Elijah," Nahri said.

Silas glared at her and puffed out his chest. "Yeah, except for probably me. He might've been great, but I'm the heir to the Summerlands."

"Right," Nahri agreed quickly.

Mikael made to step around Silas and his crew. "Are you done? We have to get to lunch."

Nahri held out an arm, stopping his movement. "You can leave when we tell you that you can leave."

"Well, I say, good riddance to Elijah," Silas said, his sneer returning. "He was up to no good."

"I don't believe that," I said.

"Well, he was," Silas snapped at me. "And I know because

my parents told me that some students were saying he was doing some wild experiments."

"Wild experiments? What does that mean?"

Mikael pushed Nahri's arm away. "Don't listen to them, Jaden."

"If he was siphoning magic, then what was he using it for?" Silas smirked. "That had to mean Elijah was into some evil stuff, you know?" Satisfaction covered his face.

"I don't believe that," I repeated, feeling defensive. "Elijah is one of the best people I know."

Silas scoffed. "You taking up for Elijah is starting to make me believe that you're just like him."

I stepped to him. "Take that back!"

"No," he spat. "He was an evil, siphoning monster, and so are you. You don't deserve to be here." He gestured at the wand I gripped in my hand. "And that bristlecone wand shouldn't have bonded with you either. It's made for someone who's heritage, like me. You're just as bad as Elijah. I'm glad he's disappeared."

I pointed my wand at him but couldn't say a spell.

Silas laughed aloud, and so did his friends. It was uneasy at first, but then they all started bellowing.

Scion ran up and pushed me aside. Anger clouded her face as she pointed her wand at Silas. "Urukpuru ga efe efe!" Clouds formed under Silas's feet, thunder sounding throughout the entire hallway. With a yelp, Silas rose to the ceiling, blasted against it, and then fell to the floor with a sickening *oof*.

"Leave him alone!" she said.

Nahri, Sean, and Erick moved quickly, brandishing their wands and pointing them at Scion.

In a flash of light, Carmine appeared out of nowhere, holding his wand aloft. *Bang, bang, bang.* Balls of flame erupted from his wand as a scowl wrapped his face.

"Enough!" he growled. "School just started!"

We all grew silent as he yelled. He sent an angry look Silas's way as he struggled up from the floor. "Mr. Rivers, take your friends and go to your next class." He turned to us now. "Mr. Powers, try not to get kicked out of magic school before it's even really begun."

I grabbed Scion's hand, and we ran to the cafeteria, Mikael following behind us.

❧

"We should talk in private," Mikael suggested after lunch, taking out his copy of *The Five Emergences, A History of Sorcery*, thumbing through it as we left the cafeteria and took the first-year staircase. "I know a good place."

Scion and I followed him, rounding a corner. "Ahh, there it is," Mikael whispered to himself. We approached a painting hanging from a wall, the image depicting a replica of the palace. He tapped his wand on it, and the image began to shimmer.

"What's this?" Scion asked.

"A meeting place," Mikael said. "They're all over the palace, and it keeps people from barging into conversations. We're not supposed to know about these until we're third-years, but I've known about them for some time."

Before we could say anything else, Mikael stepped forward and walked through the painting, the shimmering intensifying like waves.

I arched an eyebrow. "I feel like I've learned something big every single moment I've been here."

"Welcome to The Five Emergences," Scion said before dipping inside. I followed her, and for a moment, my eyesight was blinded, a cold sensation washing over me. In the next moment, I was in a warm room, a fire burning in a welcoming fireplace. Scion and Mikael were spread out on obsidian couches situated atop dark hardwood. A coffee table sat in the middle of the room.

I was tired of holding so much in; I needed to tell someone what was going on or I felt like I was going to burst. "I need to talk to y'all," I said, sitting in the middle of Scion and Mikael. "I came here for a reason." My heart beat faster and faster as I thought about what I would tell them and what I would keep to myself.

A smell of sweet oranges perfumed my nose, and I felt a deep calm settling on my shoulders. It felt like my mother. I yawned. "What's going on?"

"The meeting places always give you what you think you need most," Mikael said. "It's calming you because you need it."

I turned to Scion. "Thank you for helping me out back there with Silas."

"He's the worst," she said. "Always has been. His family tried to murder the population of Atlantis hundreds of years ago and take over the entire city. So, I have no love for the fae or the Riverses. That's why I couldn't wait to come here, actually."

"What do you mean?" I asked.

"The fae can be very . . . destructive when they want to be," Mikael pointed out. "For the most part, the supernaturals get along; it's the fae that think they should control everything."

Scion nodded in agreement. "I came here because Atlantis is just as powerful as they are. The fae tried to take our city, but we stood up to them and won. We didn't suffer any deaths in that battle, but they did. I came here to show Silas and his people that Atlantis will never back down to them. Ever."

I felt the pride dripping off her, and I loved the feeling. "Can I trust you?"

"From where I stand, me and Mikael are the only ones who even talk to you, so you'd better learn quick to trust me."

"She has a point there," Mikael said.

I sighed before beginning. "I came here for Elijah."

"Did you know he was a Sorcerer?" Scion asked.

I shook my head. "I didn't know anything about him being magical at all," I said. "But I still want to find him." At that moment, I decided against telling them about my late Outburst. Although I trusted them, I still couldn't bring myself to tell them everything. I couldn't risk pushing them away even more than my connection to Elijah had already pushed every other student in our class away. "And I don't think he was evil, or practicing siphoning magic."

Mikael pulled out a notepad from his wallet and settled it on the coffee table, along with a black pen. "I don't think this is a good idea, but if we're going to find Elijah, then we need to plan next steps to prove his innocence."

I breathed a sigh of deep relief; it wasn't often that people saw me as being truthful or as someone to follow. I was glad to see that people at least were starting to believe me.

"Let's start off with what we know," I suggested.

"We know that you and Elijah were best friends," Scion pointed out while Mikael wrote.

"And we know that Elijah helped Luxor while he was here," Mikael said, writing it down. "And, Elijah created spells and went on missions."

"Wait," I said, snapping my fingers. "If Elijah went on missions to defeat monsters, then him disappearing from the palace was probably not that suspicious to people. Right?"

"It wasn't at first," Scion said, shaking her head. "But that all changed when the entire magical world found out Carmine caught Elijah with the Ruin and then disappeared."

"Anything else we wanna add?" Mikael said, capping his pen.

"I think that's about it," I said.

"If we're going with Elijah wasn't siphoning magic and didn't cause the Ruin . . . ," Mikael began. I gave him a sharp look, and Mikael put both hands up. "No, no, I believe that Elijah is innocent!"

Scion nodded. "Me too," she reassured me. "We just need to come up with a theory of who *else* it could be."

"I think we should now add a section for suspects or people who might know something we don't know," Mikael said, uncapping the pen again and writing and underlining the word "suspects."

"Silas, maybe?" I said.

"Nah," Scion said. "He's a first-year, like us. He wouldn't know the spells to even cause the Ruin to happen."

I nodded, stifling a laugh. "Truth. I still hate him though."

Mikael giggled and pointed his pen at the paper. "So, who do we add?"

"Luxor," I said, remembering what Mikael had told me earlier. "He resigned after Elijah disappeared, right? Why would he do that?"

"That *is* suspicious," Mikael mumbled.

Scion snapped her fingers. "And what did Professor Hadiza say? She said that siphon magic is mysterious and that no one knows much about it. However, the Deterring Danger professor might, right? Elijah was brilliant, yes, but who else could teach a twelve-year-old ancient magic?"

Mikael wrote Luxor's name down.

I told Scion about the photograph Mikael and I had seen on Cayman's desk. "Professor Cayman, for sure too," I said. "He had to have enchanted that photo after I pointed it out. He obviously knows something we don't."

"Wow, I think we are in a full-blown conspiracy!" Scion said.

I nodded. "What about Carmine?"

Mikael sighed heavily. "Carmine can't be involved. Right?"

"He might not be involved, but he was the one who said Elijah was practicing illegal magic first," I said.

Scion fidgeted with her hands. "You really think the most powerful being on the planet known to magickind is somehow involved?"

"No, I don't," I responded. "But he might know more than he's letting on. He wasn't really forthcoming about . . . well, anything, when he picked me up for school. But I will give him credit for telling me most of everything later."

Mikael wrote Carmine's name down. "I don't know how we're going to get him to speak on anything, but it's worth a try."

"Wait," I said, suddenly remembering. "He said something about wanting to examine me or something."

"For what?" Mikael asked.

I hesitated, choosing my words wisely. "I don't really know. He said something about how me being from the normal world would make people treat me differently." He hadn't said it in that context, but what else could I say? I hurried on. "I could try to ask him some questions when he's doing his examination. I can try to gain his trust."

Their faces both held suspicious looks, but they didn't voice anything.

"There's something else too," I said, making a decision on the fly. If I was going to get their help, I had to show them this. I pulled out Elijah's notebook from my backpack. "I found this in his room before Carmine came to my house."

They pored over the contents of the notebook, focusing on the indecipherable language first. "I've never seen this language before," Mikael said. "And I've studied so many of them."

"Me either," Scion whispered. "And it's not in the Atlantean native tongue."

"Elijah was that good that he created his own language?" I asked.

"Looks like it. And why were you able to find it?" Mikael mused. "Someone like Elijah would *not* allow this notebook to fall into just anyone's hands. If anyone would've found it, it would have been Carmine, but you found it?"

"Maybe Elijah only wanted you to see it?" Scion said.

"And that's not all," I said, pulling out the loose sheet from the back of the notebook. "This translated when I cried before his supposed memorial."

There it was on paper, those words that had haunted me ever since I had first read them:

Jaden, I'm sorry I had to leave, but something's gone wrong.
A horrible evil is after me.
I need your help.

Mikael yelped. "So he *did* mean these writings to go to you! And this proves that he's not behind the Ruin!"

Scion stood and paced the room. "This changes so much, Jaden. Does Carmine know about this?"

I shook my head. "I told him some things, but not everything."

"We gotta find out what happened," Mikael said. "Oh my gosh, oh my gosh, oh my gosh, Elijah is innocent!"

"Told ya," I said.

"We have Elixirs tomorrow, so we should study," Scion said, checking her schedule and pulling out her dreambook. "If we're going to investigate Elijah's disappearance, then we need to know as many spells as possible."

"Good idea," I said, pulling out my own dreambook. "And I want to learn how to make my phone work in this place."

CHAPTER FIFTEEN

The next morning, we went to Elixirs, which was located in the palace kitchens. Our section of first-years trudged inside, excited whispers emanating from us all. The kitchens were modern and sleek, the scent of sugar perfuming the air. They were equipped with the best features: triple glass ovens with mechanical burners, appliances made of stainless steel, black marble floors, and multiple cooking displays with marble countertops spread throughout the room. Each display had its own oven, microwave, utensils, cast-iron skillets, burners, and large golden cauldrons with ladles connected to them. Giant windows were situated around the huge space, multicolored curtains falling to the floor.

"Only one person per display, please," a voice said. I jumped as the curtains near me fluttered in the wind and a man appeared, dressed in all black. The cape attached to his shoulders flowed in nonexistent wind. It had rubies affixed to it, shimmering in the light. He was a short man, with an angular nose, arched eyebrows, and a dreamy expression. "I am Professor Jarus Augustine."

We all stood in one spot, enraptured by him.

He clapped his hands. "One student per workstation," he repeated. "There is no need for partners in Elixirs. Your magic will only aid you when you do the work on your own. Please move quickly."

We did as we were told, and I chose a workstation near the back of the kitchens. I knew from school that sitting in the back meant that teachers wouldn't bother you too much. Mikael and Scion settled near the middle of the class.

"Elixirs are the most powerful form of magic in the known world," Professor Augustine began, his cape flowing around him as if it were caught in a vortex. "I choose to teach them like a cooking class because I quite like the euphemism. Plus, we all must eat, so why not make it fun?"

He walked around the class as he continued, waving his wand absentmindedly through the air. "Please put on the uniforms located in the cabinets underneath your display." I opened the cabinet and placed the white chef's hat on my head and the button-down coat over my school uniform. "We are going to create a sleeping elixir out of your favorite foods." With a dramatic flourish, he brought out a vial of purple liquid, smoke steaming from its closed top. "Sleeping is powerful and healing, and Sorcerers need as much as they can get. Magic is energy, you see, so you must understand that your magical ability is tied to *your* energy."

Augustine came to each of our stoves and had us peer at the vial of liquid. "This sleeping potion is nonaddicting, and you can use it for those long nights when you are up studying." He smirked. "And trust me, you *will* be studying hard here." He was right about that. Mikael, Scion, and I had studied our dreambooks for hours last night, and I felt like we had just scratched the surface; in that span I had only memorized the spells on the first five pages.

"Elixirs, like enchantments, are all about intention. And with cooking, if it tastes good, the elixir might work well. If it tastes bad . . . well . . ." Augustine completed a thumbs-down motion.

"The spell you will use for this assignment is 'mepụta ọgwụ ụra.'" He swept his wand at the board, the incantation writing itself. "Your ingredient cabinets are enchanted to correspond with your intentions, so you can cook whatever you'd like."

Justice Cameron raised his hand.

"Yes?"

"How will we know that our cooking worked?"

"Great question." Augustine raised his wand and brought it down in a vertical arch. Flames burst on each stovetop, and then cages appeared out of the smoke, mice running around inside. "You'll feed it to your mouse. If they fall asleep, it worked. Are we ready to start?"

We all mumbled a "yes."

"Good. Let's get to work. You have two hours." Instructions wrote themselves on the board when Augustine pointed to it.

I bowed my head, thinking about what I wanted to cook. As I thought hard, I realized that I didn't cook because I wasn't allowed to. My parents wouldn't even let me use the microwave without them being in the kitchen to watch me.

I do make a mean bowl of cereal. That was about it. I wondered if that would work.

I opened the cabinet beneath my stove and found a bowl, a box of frosty flakes, and a spoon. There was even a small refrigerator underneath with a carton of milk inside. Near the fridge was a vial and a little tube.

I took out the materials and placed them on top of the stove as Augustine passed by me, chuckling along the way. "Is that all, Mr . . . ?"

"Powers. And that's all I know how to make, Professor," I said. Soft laughter sounded in the room at my answer.

He shrugged as he checked in with another student. "Let's see if it works."

Insecurity gripped me. I felt like a failure, like I wasn't worthy of being in the same school Elijah once studied in.

An aroma wafted my way. It was Mikael, taking out seasoned baked chicken from his oven. He placed a thermometer inside the biggest piece, shook his head once, and then placed the platter back inside. Scion worked furiously from her display, mixing up what looked like flour and eggs in a large bowl, a sifting machine sitting next to her. Gorgona sat in a pub chair, stirring homemade spaghetti sauce into a steaming bowl of noodles. Peter was sprinkling sugar on ice cubes while Justice was kneading dough with pepperoni slices sitting on a saucer near him.

I turned my attention back to my station. *I might as well get this over with. If I fail, I fail.* But magic had a lot to do with intention. Believing was half the battle. With a sigh that helped to clear my mind, I poured the cereal into a bowl and mixed the milk with it. I took out my wand, inhaled another deep breath, and uttered, "Mepụta ọgwụ ụra." The milk bubbled a bit before settling back to normal. The smell of the cereal changed from a sweet, sugary aroma to a salty one.

"Hmm," I said, picking up my dropper and vial. After unscrewing the cap on the vial, I stirred the elixir with my wand as the instructions said, and then dipped my dropper inside the bowl, extricating the liquid. I screwed the cap on the vial and then put the dropper inside the mouse cage. It took a few licks of the salty liquid, and I stood for a couple seconds just looking at it. After about three minutes, the mouse collapsed in its cage, breathing with contentment.

"Great job!" Augustine said from the front of the room. He hadn't even been looking at me, but as soon as the mouse fell asleep, he swept over to me in a flurry of robes. "Mr. Powers, I daresay you've got it!"

I grinned as the rest of the class grumbled, Gorgona sending me a nasty look.

"Ahh!" Justice screamed from the middle of the room. I scrambled back as his cage burst open, and a mouse the size of an entire house screeched.

"No, no, no!" Augustine said with anger in his voice. The mouse screeched again as everyone yelled in terror and ran to the back of the room where I was. "Intention is the key, Mr. Cameron!" He ran and brandished his wand. "Chinwuo oke ahụ!" The mouse shrank back to normal size, and my heart calmed as Augustine cupped it from the floor and gently placed it in the pocket of his cloak. He turned to us, his once perfectly combed hair now falling into his eyes.

"Mr. Cameron, if you are unsure about your magic, then you shouldn't use it until you *are* sure," he huffed. "Mistakes happen as first-year students. But you must remember your intention." He checked his watch and clapped twice. "I think that's enough. Everyone, clean your workstations." He turned his gaze to me. "And, Mr. Powers, you may keep your vial, as you were the first one to complete *and* succeed at your elixir. Consider it your reward and passing grade for the day."

"That's not fair," I heard Peter say as I started to clean my bowl in the sink on my workstation. "He only made a bowl of cereal!"

"It's probably his connection to Elijah," Gorgona said to him. "Jaden probably weakened Justice's magic, to be honest."

"That's not true!" Mikael said as I tried to ignore the conversation. "Siphon magic doesn't work like that!"

"Cut it out, Peter and Gorgona," Scion said. "Justice failed on his own. Blame him and his intention, not Jaden." Every student in the class got quiet at that. Everyone must've heard about how Scion took on Silas. No one wanted to try her. I wondered how long they would let her take up for me.

"We don't bully in here!" Augustine barked, pointing to Gorgona and Peter. "You've both earned yourself a detention tonight after dinner. I don't care *who* you are or what family you come from." They grumbled underneath their breath, but didn't argue back.

"Mr. Powers," Augustine said as he leaned against a large refrigerator at the entrance to the kitchen. "Can I speak with you for a moment?"

I trudged up to the front, careful not to look at any of the students who hated me. Augustine pointed at the vial. "Make sure you hold on to that." I stuck it in my backpack.

Augustine folded his arms. "You *earned* that sleeping elixir; they're just jealous because you got there before they did."

I looked away from him. "Yeah, right."

"Don't let what they say stop you from realizing your destiny as a Sorcerer. I struggled when I came here for school . . . oh . . . many moons ago, now. But I stuck it out and I became a professor here, excelling in every magic system taught. And you will do the same, I'm sure. The sleeping potion is a hard elixir to master for any first-year."

"But I did it!" I grinned.

"You did, and you know who else mastered it?"

I ventured a guess. "Elijah."

"*Before* the rumors started." He leaned closer to me and whispered, "You know what I think? I think you're *just* like him, just as powerful. Sorcerers from the normal world usually are because they have something to prove. I believe you have something to prove, Mr. Powers."

Relief coursed through my body as he spoke to me. "Thank you, Professor Augustine."

"Don't thank me," he said, placing a hand on my shoulder. "Learn how to thank yourself."

And with that, he slunk into the shadow between the wall and the fridge, disappearing into nothing.

CHAPTER SIXTEEN

After dinner, we returned to our dormitory, Scion going into the girls' portion on the other side of the staircase.

Mikael talked a mile a minute as we prepared for bed, the sky darkening as he spoke.

"Can you believe it? You won the sleeping vial!"

I sat on my bed reading my dreambook, mumbling spells to myself, ignoring Mikael.

He spun around the room like a tornado, holding his wand aloft, making blasting sounds with his mouth. "Pretty soon, I'll be able to take on Silas. I just *know* it! Give me like . . . I don't know, a month or so, and I know I'll be better than him!" He twirled again in his pajamas as I continued to read. "Jaden, you okay?"

"I'm good. I'm just studying."

"I can't believe you won!"

"I *earned* it," I said, much angrier than I intended.

Mikael stopped twirling and stood in front of me, his eyes growing sad. "I—I didn't mean it like that, man. I'm actually glad you won it. You deserve it."

I sighed. "I know, Mikael, and I'm sorry. I'm just mad that I have to prove myself here, that everyone hates me."

"Scion and I don't hate you."

"I know y'all don't. And I love that. It's just weird that everyone else does. I mean, Justice is Black like me, and so is Sean, Silas's friend. You'd think they'd at least treat me better, Justice especially, since he's in our first-year section."

"I know," Mikael said, putting his wand on the bookshelf near his bed. "And I'm sorry." He took out his notepad and carried it over to me. "Do you have anyone else you want to add to the list?"

"Not yet," I said, shaking my head. "Maybe I'll know more in the next couple of days."

"Okay," he said, placing it back on his bookshelf and getting into bed. "Another long day tomorrow. Good night, Jaden."

"Good night," I said, but he was already asleep before I even said the word. I spent the next hour studying from my books, and then I turned off the lamp.

Before drifting off to sleep, I sent a mental prayer to Elijah, hoping he'd hear me.

I don't know where you are, but I will find you.

After two weeks of classes and studying more than I ever thought possible, our schedules changed.

"Deterring Danger is our first class of the day," Scion said, looking at the wrinkled parchment that appeared in our rooms this morning.

I yawned as we took the first-year staircase down to the bottom of the palace. Aibell had decided last night to scream and scream for hours, until I learned a Silence enchantment that drowned her out. But by the time I mastered it, it was already three o'clock in the morning.

Deterring Danger's location was written as "palace entrance," and that was it. We stood there for a while as the rest of our first-year section appeared.

The sound of heels clacking on marble turned my attention behind me. Stepping out of the shadows was Professor Cinxia Menifee, shades covering her eyes.

"Deterring Danger will commence in a secret location," she said in a curt voice, taking out her wand, her muscular arms bulging as she did. "It's time you start getting physical. You've sat in comfy desks for two weeks, and now you need to get moving." I wanted to point out that Cayman had us flying in the air, changing our clothes, and traveling all over the palace, but Menifee didn't seem like someone who tolerated students talking back.

Before anyone could say anything, she waved her wand in the air and whispered a spell.

"Whoa!" I screamed as the floor opened underneath us and we fell through it. I closed my eyes as pressure built up in my ears. I kept them closed until I felt the sensation of slowing down. When I opened them, my boots settled on soft sand, the sky even bluer than the sky outside the palace. I peered into the distance, shading my eyes against the heat. Birds flew, but they were fuzzy, as if someone had drawn them and hadn't finished yet.

We were standing on a beach of sorts, a blue body of water spreading from left to right in front of us. Targets rose from the sand, a red dot in the middle of each of them.

Menifee paced in front of us with her wand, her face stern and commanding.

"Welcome to Deterring Danger," she began.

Mikael raised his hand. "Where are we?"

"Inside the palace, of course," she said. "Being a Sorcerer is not just about how you create or cast spells; it's also about how you defend yourself." Her expression turned angry. "Do you want to graduate from The Five Emergences just to be killed by a horde of zombies? What about being ripped apart by feral vampires? What if you're drowned by a singing, vengeful siren?" She stopped and showed us huge scars on her arms. "These were given to me by one of the wild Nemean lions. It took large chunks of me with it before I killed it."

My eyes widened as she spoke, fear trickling through my entire body. *What have I just gotten myself into?*

"Deterring Danger is all about how you defend yourself

from supernatural beasts and powerful, evil Sorcerers." She paused when we gasped. "What? You thought all Sorcerers were good people?" She laughed. "Yes, when you graduate . . . *if* you graduate, you're going to be faced with all sorts of terrible things, even in the normal world. You need to learn how to protect yourself."

She guided us over to the targets and placed one person per target, a few feet away from one another.

"You're not only aiming at something," she explained as she lifted her wand to her own target. "You're learning how to use the Blasting spell, to subdue your enemy." She flicked her wand and spoke, "Gbarie ihe mgbaru ọsọ." Her target exploded in pieces, flame and smoke licking the air.

We all jumped and screamed.

"That's the spell you'll learn today," she said, ignoring our screams. "And it's not as easy as you think. Your aim must be true before we move on to the second part of the lesson."

Scion raised her hand. "What's that?"

Menifee swept her wand in the sky; the air shimmered like heat before a large labyrinth appeared where the trees grew. After, she pointed at grains of sand and said, "Gbanwee ghọọ mpi ịnyịnya." Dirt flew in the air, transforming into white unicorns, golden horns burrowed in their foreheads, their heads surrounded by purple hair.

She frowned at our yells of awe. "You're happy now, but you won't be when you finish your Blasting spells." She pointed her wand at the labyrinth, and the unicorns ran into the woods and disappeared inside. A roar sounded on the beach, so loud that our clothes rippled. "Your task is to save the unicorns from the minotaur inside."

Pure horror coursed through me as everyone gasped.

"We're not strong enough!" I said. "We're just first-years!"

"You only aren't if you *think* so," Menifee said, deepening her frown. "Now, let's get started! The first one that saves their unicorn gets extra credit." She swept her wand at the ground, and army fatigues appeared near our feet. "And put these on first. No need to sully your good Sorcerer clothes when you're being trained to be warriors now!"

We didn't even have time to deal with our horror before we began. After putting on my soldier uniform, I lifted my wand almost immediately to my target, shouting the Blasting spell. *Boom.* The air exploded around it, but the target did not. I tried again, but nothing. After fifteen minutes, no one had been able to aim well enough to disintegrate the bullseye.

Menifee stood behind me after what seemed like my hundredth try, pulling my wand even higher. "Just like with other spells," she whispered, "focus on your *intention*. Visualize what you want the spell to do, and then actually *want* to be successful. Once you master your fear, you'll master the spell." She pushed my wand even higher. "Also, your line of sight isn't linear. Push above the target and it'll explode."

"I think what's stopping me is the fact that I have to kill a minotaur."

"Hmm."

With that, she strolled away to the next student while I continued to practice. I emptied my mind and focused on my intention, trying to visualize what I wanted to happen. A blasting tone sounded in my ear, and I turned to see Scion take off into the woods first, her target torn into pieces.

Focus on yourself, I thought as I aimed again at my target, narrowing my eyes as I raised my wand an inch or so higher. "Gbarie ihe mgbaru ọsọ!" I jerked a bit when my target exploded.

"Let's go, Mr. Powers!" Menifee barked. I faced the labyrinth now, my heart beating so fast that I felt hard pressure.

I ran across the beach, right as Peter's target exploded. He ran after me, trying to keep up. When I went inside the woods, the labyrinth rose in front of me, black, menacing, a large opening set in its middle. Peter crashed through the wood right behind me, and once he saw me, he growled and burst into flames. "Move, siphoner."

Who knew a seraphim could be so scary?

I ran ahead of him. But no matter how much faster I ran, the labyrinth door opening seemed to be getting farther and farther away. "What is going on?" Water spread as a trickle in front of me at first, and then enlarged until it was a deep river, the minotaur's roar in the maze ahead keeping me present.

Okay, Jaden, I thought to myself as I waded into the cold water. *You got this. You can do this. Make Elijah proud.*

Splash. Right when I was about to dive, I saw Scion jumping out of the water on the other end, the gills on her neck suctioning in and out. *Of course, she's a pro at this.*

I jumped into the brown water, submerging myself to get used to the coolness. As fast as I could, I swam across the river until my hand hit the sandy side of the next shore. When I jumped out, a tall wooden plank rose in front of me with hand-holds bored into it. Scion scrambled over the top of it, disappearing onto the other side.

Without questioning it, I heaved myself on the open grooves and climbed until I stalled in the middle, my breath coming in ragged streams. I rested there for a while, laying my head against the coolness of the wood. I didn't even care that Peter had begun to climb behind me.

"I can't do this," I whispered. "I can't do this. I'm so tired. This is just too hard." *But you can do this, Jaden. There's nothing to stop you from completing this course but yourself.*

Peter jumped in front of me, smirking as he passed.

"Jaden!" I turned to see Mikael jumping out of the river and running over to the wooden wall. "You have to keep going!"

I can do this. I know I can.

With huge effort, I kept climbing upward as Mikael called encouragement my way. I coasted the top of the wall, just in time to see Peter jumping to the bottom. I gulped. There were no hand- or footholds on this side. After taking a deep breath, I jumped to the ground. When I touched down, a bridge appeared out of thin air in front of me, made with planks on the bottom and hanging ropes at the top. Peter was just a few paces in front of me, moving swiftly toward the labyrinth opening.

Without thinking, I jumped onto the first plank, daring myself not to look behind me and definitely not below me, where there was nothing but air. It was like I had climbed from the sand to a mountaintop, and I was walking through open sky. I kept moving across the planks, one of them in the middle coming loose from rot. I tripped once, my hands brushing against cool air before I stood up again, the ropes helping me regain my balance.

I kept moving, holding on to the ropes and jumping over any gaps until I dropped down on the other side, right in front of the labyrinth, moving so fast that I had caught up with Peter. He ran when he saw me, but I caught up with him again, and we both burst through the maze right when the minotaur roared.

Two paths diverged in the dark tangle of weeds.

Peter took the left. "*Don't* follow me," he snapped. "You stay on your side, and I'll stay on mine."

He didn't have to tell me twice. I ran to the right, fighting my way through thick brambles, weeds, and vines. Thorns snatched at my fatigues as I went, ripping them in small patches. Cuts appeared on my exposed skin, blood forming and then congealing as soon as it hit exposed air.

The minotaur bellowed in the distance, but I did my best to clamp down on my fear.

A loud whinny cut through the noise as I rounded a corner and came into a clearing. A unicorn stood in front of me, its golden horn shining in the darkness. As soon as I approached, the minotaur appeared out of the shadows, holding a large axe in its hands, its face that of a humongous bull, its feet thick as tree trunks. It towered over me, its two horns spiked, its face gnarled. It bellowed so loudly that the air blasted me, sending me careening to the side. My back hit the brambles behind me, and my fatigues became tangled.

"You . . . are scary," I managed to say before it came at me with full speed, holding its axe aloft as the unicorn skittered away.

"Forget this," I said, turning around to run back through the path's opening, but thick vines covered it as soon as I was about to step through.

"Oh, crap," I said as the large, thick gleaming axe came down. I scrambled away just in time.

"Gbarie ihe mgbaru ọsọ," I squeaked, holding my wand aloft. An explosion racked the space, dust falling to the ground, but that was it. The minotaur still stood, unharmed and untouched. I ran as the axe came down again. "Please get me outta here, please get me outta here," I moaned, but nothing happened.

The beast roared and came for me again, swiping down. The axe burrowed and got stuck in the ground, which gave me time to move away and aim my wand at it again.

"Gbarie ihe mgbaru ọsọ!" I said again, this time more confident. But my aim wasn't true. The minotaur blasted backward, hitting the opposite wall of brambles, but still very much alive. I directed my wand at the stuck axe; it broke apart, slicing in two as the spell crashed into it. At least with it out of the picture, I wouldn't be worried about getting carved in half.

The minotaur stood and stalked me, walking back and forth in front of me. "I destroyed your weapon," I said, pounding my chest. "Come at me now."

The minotaur roared and jumped across the space toward me. "No, I didn't mean come at me like *that*." I pointed my wand at it and closed my eyes, casting blindly. A bellow of pain met my ears, and I opened my eyes. The beast was rolling across the ground, holding its bleeding foot.

"I'm sorry, I'm sorry," I said as I bounded across the clearing to stand in front of the scared unicorn. I petted its head and I jumped on its back. "I could've killed you, but I didn't," I pleaded as the minotaur continued to yelp in pain, hoping that it wouldn't follow me. And that it could understand my language.

The opening appeared in the vines, and the unicorn jumped through, racing toward the maze's entrance.

We stood outside the labyrinth's entrance, all of us bloody and beaten and bruised. The unicorns had transformed back into grains of sand.

Menifee stood in front of us, smiling wide. "You have all completed your mission," she said, before stopping at a shivering student. "Except for Cecil. He almost drowned in the river, and I had to come save him." No one laughed at him; no one made a sound. The fear had been overpowering for me, and it was understandable to me that one of us wouldn't make it through.

"One of you completed the mission faster than everyone else," she said, stopping in front of Scion. "I should've known a goddess would succeed where others failed."

Scion smiled in response. "It was no biggie."

"You'll receive your own unicorn as a gift," she said. "It'll be delivered to you when you return to school."

"I can't believe we had to hurt something," I muttered. To my surprise, everyone else mumbled their agreement. Who knew that fighting a minotaur would bring the people who hated me all together?

Menifee tossed me an uninterested look. "I had to make it real, Mr. Powers, or you wouldn't have taken my class seriously. This is all a simulation." She pointed her wand at the labyrinth, and it shimmered out of existence, then returned, like haze in a bright sun.

"As was the minotaur. Nothing was truly hurt in this experience."

We all gasped, and Cecil stepped forward, his eyes full of anger. "You've gotta be kidding me! You mean I almost drowned for nothing?"

Menifee shrugged. "You'll be okay. A Sorcerer must be prepared for any and everything."

With a swipe of her wand, we lifted from the ground, thundering through the air at warp speed until we stood in an empty classroom with two doors. Menifee was like whiplash; one moment I thought I was going to die, the next moment I was told it was all a simulation, and in the last moment, I wanted to lash out at her, but we were tumbling back to the real world before any of us really could.

"Class is over," Menifee announced as she walked through the door that led to her office. "You may leave."

As the students streamed out of the second door, a thought hit me. Menifee had seemed interested in my theories about Elijah. Maybe she knew something more that I didn't know?

"I'm gonna talk to Menifee," I said to Scion and Mikael.

"We have to get to lunch," Scion said.

"I don't care about lunch right now," I responded. "I'll just see you guys later."

"But why talk to her now?" Mikael protested, flicking mud off his arms. "She didn't tell you anything the first time you spoke with her."

"Don't worry about it," I told them, marching toward her office. "I'll figure out something."

I closed the office door behind me so they couldn't stop me. "Hello, Professor Menifee." She sat at her desk, her forearms bulging as she sipped from a cup of tea. It didn't seem like she had changed the furnishings at all—pictures of Luxor and his accomplishments still decorated the entire oval-shaped room, hanging on the walls and sitting on her desk.

"Mr. Powers, how can I help you?" she said, taking another sip.

"I talked with Professor Cayman about Elijah."

Her eyes narrowed as she motioned for me to sit. "Tell me more." She didn't seem impressed; no, if anything, she seemed *intrigued*.

I sat. "Cayman pretended he didn't know anything about Elijah. But I saw a picture of Elijah with Luxor on his desk."

She sighed. "Like I said earlier, what are the odds that you and Elijah would *both* have magic? Seems . . . defying odds, doesn't it?"

I tensed. "That's all I have for now. Do you have anything else?"

"I don't know much," she said, getting up to pour another cup of hot tea and offering it to me. "All I know is that . . . I'm not sure I should be speaking on this."

"But he was my best friend!"

She nodded. "I know the love between friends. And I also know that you came in second today during our lesson. That was a feat that I thought a supernatural would do, not someone from the normal world."

I shrugged. "I don't want to fail out of school."

"Because you think Elijah's innocent?" When I nodded yes, she sighed. "What else do you want to know?"

"I want to know more about Luxor."

She sat. "When Luxor resigned, I applied for his job. I have my suspicions about him, but that's all I can say for now."

"What are you saying?" I took a sip of my tea, not because I wanted it, but because I needed to do something with my fidgeting hands.

She frowned. "What I *can* say is that Elijah is a child." She lifted an eyebrow.

My mind whirled with the possibilities, until it settled on something I had been missing. "Wait. Mikael said that Luxor resigned after Elijah disappeared. Do you know where he is now? Could I speak with him?"

She shook her head. "Unfortunately, no. No one has seen Luxor since he left the school. When Elijah disappeared, he disappeared too."

It was my turn to frown. That was pretty suspicious. "And Carmine, the greatest Sorcerer to ever exist, can't find either one of them?"

"Nope."

That could only mean one thing; Luxor *had* to have been the one siphoning magic. Menifee had just said that Elijah was a child, which would imply that he was too young to know that type of magic . . . so that meant that Luxor was the real culprit. And what if Elijah had disappeared because he had found out the truth, but he knew no adult would believe him? Just like my parents never believed me.

I stifled a gasp. And what if Luxor had resigned because he wanted to find Elijah before Elijah could reveal his deep, dark secret? No *wonder* Elijah had left me that note! He was trying to tell me that someone was after him, and that someone was Luxor!

"I still don't believe Elijah is behind the Ruin," I whispered.

"I appreciate your fondness for Mr. Williams," Menifee said, her eyebrows arching. "But, tell me, did he tell you about magic school? Did he share with you what he was doing here?"

"N-no?"

"Then with all due respect, you don't know *what* Elijah was up to. Plus, you're too young to understand the intricacies of our world. You did well today, but that doesn't mean you're ready to face anything evil, especially not an evil like Elijah and the Ruin."

Anger burned in me. Why did all adults act like I couldn't do anything?

"I can prove myself."

Menifee chuckled. "Okay, Mr. Powers. I believe you. But now I think it's time you get to lunch. Talk to me in a few years after you've mastered some stronger spells."

"But—"

"That will be all, Mr. Powers."

CHAPTER SEVENTEEN

The next morning, Aibell screamed us awake and pushed the door open, her hair hanging over her face, her feet dragging against the floor as she floated.

"Aibell!" I screamed, pulling off the covers. "What do you want?"

"Get out!" Mikael said, throwing a pillow at her.

"Did I scare you?" She grinned.

"Nope. What do you want?" I said again.

Her eyes fell. "Guess not." She handed an envelope to me. "It's from Headmaster Carmine."

The envelope opened on its own when Aibell slammed the door behind her.

"I wonder what it's about?" Mikael said, getting out of his bed.

I read it aloud.

Hello, Mr. Powers. Before your classes begin today, please come to my office.
We will begin our investigation.

I smiled. "He wants to see me for that study I told you about."

Mikael put a finger to his lips. "Maybe it's time to question Carmine? He was on our list."

I nodded. "I'll try." I stood and made my way to our bathroom. "I'll be back, and I'll tell you all about it."

❧

When I made it to Carmine's office, his voice sounded through the closed door.

"Mr. Powers, you may enter."

Carmine sat on his desk with wand in hand, twirling it thoughtfully.

"You have no genetic predisposition to magic, Mr. Powers. You should not be a Sorcerer. We need to figure out how you obtained your magic so that we can learn to deal with it. I wanted to wait until you've immersed yourself here before we began."

I nervously twisted my wand in my hand. "I love it here." *Minus the bullying and Silas and his friends.*

Carmine nodded. "Most students say the same thing." He pointed his wand to the seat in front of him, and I sat. "We must begin our investigation. Do I have your consent?"

"C-consent for what?" I stammered.

"To peruse through your mind."

"Does that hurt?"

"It does. There's no sugarcoating it." Carmine shrugged. "But that's the price we'll have to pay if we are to know what happened to you. It's probably the only way we will know what really happened to Elijah. Your mind is most likely hiding memories that you don't even remember."

"Do it," I whispered, the concern for myself gone now. If enduring pain was what I had to do to find Elijah, I would take it. "Look into my mind."

"Very well." He swept his wand around himself once and then pointed it at my forehead; a heavy pressure fell on my chest immediately.

"Banye n'ime n'uche."

A cobalt stream of light erupted from his wand and touched my forehead. A great agony racked my body until I was convulsing, my stomach caving inward and outward. The feeling of fire licked on my every limb. I screamed when I couldn't take it anymore.

And then that was it. The pain disappeared as quickly as it had appeared. And I had disappeared too. I floated in a dark space, a void of some sort, my eyesight gone. But it wasn't scary; it was surprisingly comfortable and soothing, like someone was holding me in their arms, close to their chest. I became lost in that comfort, snuggling in the darkness, loving that I seemed to have no body, like I was floating in warmness. I even forgot why I had come here. I wanted to stay here, forever and ever.

"Jaden."

It was Elijah's voice, bringing me back to the present.

A pinprick of light floated in front of me, and I concentrated on it. It expanded until a full black-and-white image came forth, like I was in an old movie theater. The image split into fourths, four different movies playing. The first was of me and Elijah when we were ten, playing hide-and-seek in his house.

"Jaden, imma count to ten, and that's all the time you got!" Elijah said with a huge smile on his face. I stormed downstairs when he closed his eyes to begin counting, but just as I shut the door, Elijah took out his wand and waved it in the air. When he began to count, the numbers came out of his mouth slow like molasses, giving me even more time to find a spot to hide. When he moved to the door to find me, it was like he was walking underwater. "I'm gonna find you!" he said, turning the knob.

He loved me enough to give me time.

The second image began to play now, black-and-white shadows dancing over each other as the picture came into clear view.

"Go to your room, Jaden! And tell Elijah it's time to go home," Mama yelled at a younger me, around nine. I marched upstairs, tears rushing from my eyes. When I slammed my door, the memory changed, and Daddy walked into the living room and gave Mama a hug.

"I just don't know what to do about him and Elijah," Mama said. "He gets so upset when we separate him from Elijah. But Elijah can't be his only friend."

"The only thing we can do is try our best," Dad said.

"I just hope that one day Jaden understands."

I hadn't seen or heard this conversation—I had just been told to go to my room to tell Elijah he needed to leave. The image changed, and there I was in my room, sitting on my bed and crying.

"You have to go home," I said. "They don't want me hanging around you no more. But I just don't know why. Did I do something bad?"

Elijah stood with his hands in his pockets, chewing his lower lip. He knelt beside me and wrapped warm hands around me, whispering something I hadn't remembered. Now, I recognized it as a spell. "You didn't do anything wrong, Jaden." After he spoke, I fell asleep, and he disappeared in a shower of bright colors.

He loved me enough to take my pain away.

I turned my attention to the third black-and-white movie. It depicted different flashes of Elijah and me when he came home the first summer break from Hamilton. We'd swum in the Potomac River underneath the Arlington Memorial Bridge, sneaking away from our parents. It was totally dangerous and illegal, but we didn't care. This time, I could see Elijah take out his wand and point it at the sun so it would shine brighter and longer. I could see him whispering spells that created smoky barriers around us so that we wouldn't be caught. I even saw him point his wand at the back of my neck as we swam, and watched how an orange light encircled us, allowing us to swim deeper and longer.

He loved me enough to make me part of his world.

And then there was the last black-and-white movie. It was of the day I had my Outburst. It showed me in Elijah's room, poring over the notebook and the loose sheet with his note. I watched myself cry until a tear dropped from my eyes to the pages, causing Elijah's words to translate. And then I fainted until Dad came to pick me up and carry me to the car, where I had my Outburst.

He loved me enough to leave me a message.

"Jaden, I think it's time to come back."

I could have stayed there for a million years, looking at these movies and memories over and over again. They were mine, and they were his too. But, there was a greater purpose for me.

With great difficulty, I turned from the movies and returned to the darkness.

To the void.

Tears were falling from Carmine's eyes as I returned to the present.

I wiped my own eyes, not knowing that I had been crying too.

"Are you okay?" Carmine asked.

I nodded. "I think I am."

"Good," Carmine said, taking a blue handkerchief out of his shirt pocket and dotting at his tears. He handed another one to me.

"Why were the memories different?" I said, wiping my eyes. "I remember some of it, but I couldn't have heard my parents speaking or seen what Elijah was doing."

"The brain is not your mind, Mr. Powers," Carmine said.

"What does that mean?"

"It means that the inner part of you, that part that *thinks*, that voice that you hear, is part of your mind. It is your consciousness. And when you dream, that is your subconscious at work. However, everything you do, everything you experience, everything that happens around you, is recorded by your brain. So, while you may have not seen everything that happened, it is still part of the core of your memories. Your brain is way more powerful than you think."

That made total sense to me, especially after seeing Elijah whisper spells. I hadn't seen him speak them, but I had *felt* them even though I didn't know what was going on.

"My . . . magic," I whispered, my mind blown.

Carmine nodded. "I saw. You're truly remarkable."

"So, what happened? Did you find out anything?"

"Inheritance magic," he said, taking a deep breath. A look of awe settled in his gaze as he appraised me. "I feel so foolish. I should've *known*."

"What's that?"

"It's when a prospective Sorcerer inherits magic from someone powerful. But we've only *speculated* that that could happen. We've never actually seen it done. Most Sorcerers can't change a normal person into a Sorcerer—even *I* can't do that. Either you have magic or you don't. And you don't have magic; at least, you didn't have any before you inherited it from Elijah. From the best I can surmise, when you cried over his letters, the tears gave you his magic."

"He gave me a piece of his magic?"

Carmine shrugged. "Or *all* of it. Inheritance magic is so rare that it's probably only appeared once or twice in the history of the universe, so I only know what I've read. You received magic from your friend in some way that is yet to be determined, which caused your Outburst."

"He gave me a piece of or all of his magic?" I said, confused. "Does that mean that Elijah is no longer a Sorcerer, or he's not as powerful? Does that mean he's weakened?" If so, did that also mean that he was hurt, somehow, that he *really* needed me since I now had his magic?

"I don't think he's weakened," Carmine answered. "I have a feeling he's as powerful as he's always been, if not *more* powerful. To transfer magic to someone who isn't inherently magic—such as yourself—is a great feat beyond my own understanding. Greater magic than even I possess."

"What do you mean?"

He appraised me again, looking me up and down. "I . . . I don't know. You really are a marvel."

The weight in my chest began to subside now, as a slight

relief replaced it. I didn't know all the rules for magic or anything like that, but what I did know was that Elijah wasn't weakened, wasn't in pain as he waited on me to help him.

Carmine shrugged again. "I'll need to do more research. I just don't know. Inheritance magic is so hard to understand, and you're definitely a mystery." He jumped off the desk and came face-to-face with me, his eyes boring into mine. "But what we do know right now is that Elijah had something to do with it. Your tears had something to do with it. Did Elijah give you a portion of his magic through your tears? Interesting theory, but I'm just not sure right now."

I thought hard, but no other answers could come to me. We were closer to an answer, but still not quite there yet.

Carmine waved a hand. "Either way, Elijah has something to do with why you're here, and we need to get to the bottom of it. You may leave."

I stood as Carmine swept behind his desk. "What does that mean, 'why you're here'? We have to find Elijah!"

"You may go, Mr. Powers. I need to do some research into what I've seen in your memories."

I resisted the urge to stomp my foot. "But they're *my* memories! I should be helping you look for him, or researching with you! You wouldn't have access to them without me. I need to be doing something! I'm learning so much here, and Elijah is the reason why. He should be here with me, seeing all of the progress I've made!"

Carmine sighed and sat in his palatial chair. "Do you not think I'm doing all I can to find Mr. Williams?"

"You're not moving fast enough!" I said, balling my fists.

"And you're wasting time by arguing with me when I could be working. Trust me, the greatest Sorcerer minds are looking for Elijah, Mr. Powers."

"Obviously they're not that great if you needed a twelve-year-old kid to help you!"

This was going nowhere. I turned on my heels, walked out of his office, and slammed the door on my way out.

If Carmine wasn't going to help me, I would help myself.

And one thing was clear from learning about Inheritance magic; if Elijah had somehow given me a portion of his magic, then he must have done it for a reason.

I intended to find out what that reason was.

CHAPTER EIGHTEEN

I debated whether I should tell Mikael and Scion about my Inheritance magic as I sat next to them for breakfast after leaving Carmine's office. His behavior confused me; we'd finally found out how I got my magic, but I was now barred from helping him with the search for Elijah.

Mostly, I was disappointed and sad.

I did my best to clear my mind and told Mikael and Scion everything that happened with Carmine, minus my knowledge of Inheritance magic.

Mikael's spoon fell into the milk of his cereal as I finished my story.

"That's . . . a lot," he said, his mouth wide. "I'm not sure I would have let anyone see my memories."

Scion pointed across the cafeteria where Silas and his friends were eating and sending us death stares. Silas's nose was still swollen purple from her spell. "At least we have that."

"I thought the memory investigation would help us," I said, shaking my head. "But now . . . now I'm just confused."

"What do you want to do now?" Scion asked, taking a bite from a bagel smeared with grape jelly.

"Carmine isn't gonna help me," I said, taking a sip from my orange juice. "That means we have to do our own research. I think we should go to the library soon to do some reading." I paused for a moment. "Wait, does the school even have a library?"

Scion laughed, flipping her hair behind her back. "Of course it does! Why wouldn't it? The Five Emergences is the greatest magical place on Earth!"

Mikael patted my arm. "It's okay. You're new. You'll learn."

I narrowed my eyes as they both laughed to their hearts' content.

The next day, our schedules changed again, and a new class appeared, Metamorphosis.

"Oh, yeah," Mikael said, rubbing his hands together as we walked down the first-year staircase to class. "I've been waiting for this since arriving here."

"Metamorphosis is what I *do*," Scion said as her hair grew longer and her face turned a deep shade of green. "I am from the sea, you know."

"You're happy now, but you won't be when you see this," I said, pointing at the parchment in my hands as we reached the bottom of the staircase. "Look at who the class is with."

Scion sighed as she read. "It's with the second section of first-years."

"Which means Silas will be there," I said.

"Can we ever get a break?" Mikael groaned.

"We've beaten him and his friends once," I said, strolling into an open doorway. "And we can do it again."

Like Deterring Danger, the class was empty of desks and bookshelves. Students packed inside like sardines, each section present. We stood for a while, speaking among ourselves. Silas, of course, arrived last with his friends, a black streak coursing through his emerald hair, his purple eyes enchanted to look a mixture of red and green. Everyone grew quiet as he slid in.

I rolled my eyes as the students reacted to him like he was royalty. Which he was. But whatever.

"I bet he won't remind people we clobbered him a few weeks ago," I whispered to Scion who tried her best to hold in her laughter.

"What was that?" Silas said, looking my way.

"You heard what I said," I responded, gripping my wand. The class started to whisper as we faced each other. I wasn't really looking for a fight, but I was down for one.

"That's the fae prince!" Gorgona gasped, her eyes widening, her hair wriggling as her eyes went from me to Silas and back again.

"I don't care."

An icy silence settled over the room.

"Welcome to Metamorphosis," a voice said, breaking the quiet. A woman stepped into the room, holding a pink wand. "I'm Professor Trisi Genesis." She smiled at me and Silas. "I hope I wasn't interrupting anything important."

"No, Professor," Silas said, a bright smile stretching from left to right on his face. I rolled my eyes again.

She gestured at the streak in his hair. "I like that look on you. Someone's been paying attention in Enchantment."

"Always," he said.

With a flourish, Genesis walked to the middle of the class, and we crowded around her as she pulled out a sack of emerald bracelets from a satchel she was holding. "Metamorphosis is along the line of casting enchantments, but slightly different. The spells you'll be learning with me allow you to change living things into anything that exists in our magical world or the normal world." She pushed the bracelets our way. "All first-years need one of these. Take one and wrap it around your wrist."

"What do they do?" Justice asked as he took one.

"They're transformation bracelets," Genesis said. "We require that every Sorcerer—no matter if they live in the magical world or normal world—wear one of these at all times."

I took one and wrapped it around my wrist; it immediately grew hot and burrowed into my skin, smoke rising in the air.

Across the room everyone yelped as the bracelets left a faint scar on our wrists.

"Once you put them on, you can never take them off. We track every spell, and specifically every metamorphosis spell, *and* the location in which it is cast," Genesis said, proceeding to step out into the hallway. "Now, the bulk of our class will take place in the dungeons' underground pool. Follow me, please."

We spilled out into the hallway and walked.

"I just thought of something," I whispered to Mikael and Scion from our spot in the back as we went through an opening in the wall that led to the palace dungeons. "If our bracelets track every spell and its location, how does the school not know where Luxor and Elijah are?"

Mikael and Scion shrugged, but Genesis unwittingly answered my question as the class approached a huge pool the size of a sea, smoke rising from its depths. "You won't be able to take off your bracelets without express permission from a professor here." She turned to us, her gray cape swishing around her, her gaze intense. "And that almost never happens, since only a few of us know the spell for that—even I don't know it. The standard rule is 'don't even try.'"

"What if Luxor knows the spell?" I whispered.

Scion arched an eyebrow. "Not sure that makes sense."

"Why doesn't it? He disappeared right around the time Elijah did."

"Because he disappeared after Elijah did. That would mean that Luxor was helping Elijah *before* then, right?"

Mikael nodded, seemingly agreeing with her.

"Then maybe he was. Or he's the real person behind the Ruin, and not Elijah," I said.

Genesis clapped her hands. "Let's begin our lesson." She swept her wand around her head, spoke a spell I didn't catch, and then pointed the wand at Peter. He screamed once, burst into flames, and then he shrank to the floor, turning into a gray shark.

We all yelled—and some students cursed—at the sight and jumped backward as Peter shuffled to the edge of the pool and slithered in, disappearing into the water.

"We're learning *that*?" Justice screamed. Looks of horror passed through every face except for Silas's. An amused smirk played around his mouth.

Genesis nodded. "Yes. Now, everyone, wade into the water and let's practice your first metamorphosis spell."

"But Peter's in there!" Gorgona said. "He could eat us!"

Genesis pointed her wand at the water, and it roiled in waves before a screaming Peter blasted out of the pool and fell onto the dungeon's floor. "Not anymore. Now, let's start!"

I took off my cape, boots, and socks, not giving myself time to psych myself out from what I needed to do. But as I waded into the warm water, I couldn't help but snicker when Genesis remarked to herself, "First-years can be such weaklings. I don't even know why Carmine allowed Metamorphosis to be taught to them this year."

"Whoa," I said as soon as I started to tread water, thankful that I knew how to swim. Although we were in a pool, it seemed to expand as I swam, pushing outward to all sides. In a span of a few seconds, the dungeons all but disappeared, leaving us in what seemed like an ocean of thrashing water. A wave crashed against me, and the taste of salt invaded my mouth.

Every student became pinpricks as the seconds deepened into minutes, large spaces of water dividing us. A voice boomed in my mind now, but it was not painful, not like when Carmine investigated my memories.

"I know that this is overwhelming," Genesis said. "But today's class is a test in fortitude. Be aware, when you transform, your mind will transform too, which is another reason why your bracelets are tracked—so I can always find you." She spoke the spell we would use. "Now, clear your mind of all distractions and change yourself."

I gripped my wand tight and did my best to clear my mind like she said. It was a hard thing to do. But Elijah had to have mastered the spell, right? He couldn't have defeated the kraken without using one like it.

I took a deep breath and swept my wand around my head. "Gbanwee ghọọ akụm."

Nothing happened. I tried again. Still nothing.

Genesis spoke to me. "Mr. Powers, clear your mind. Stop overthinking and focus on your *intention*. No worries if you don't get it on your first try, but you must complete the change to get your passing score for today."

You can do this; you can do this. It wasn't exactly "clearing my mind" like Genesis spoke of, but it at least got to the intention part.

"Gbanwee ghọọ akụm."

Without warning, I shrank and dove underneath the water, waves washing over my hands. Wait, no, they weren't hands; they were fins, the right one somehow still holding on to my wand. My nose elongated, and my eyes pulled to the sides of my head. My legs disappeared, and a long tail appeared, swishing faster and faster through the water. When I opened my mouth, water and salt entered, but I did not feel like I was drowning. It felt like there was oxygen in the water, helping me to breathe.

I swam deeper into the ocean's depths, my mind going almost blank as the waters darkened. Even the thoughts of Elijah subsided somewhat, and I became one with my surroundings. It was a peaceful experience, swimming the only urge I had. It could have been thirty minutes, or it could have been hours, but my animal mind wouldn't allow me to process the passage of time.

The waters grew even darker as I swam deeper, the blueness of the surface turning to emerald green. When I had completely forgotten who I was, something hard bumped into me, bringing me back to the present. I swished in the water and turned around over and over until I got a glimpse of who or what had hit me.

Silas swam above me in human form, a bubble encircling his head, his aura red. He sliced through the water with his wand, bubbles leaving his mouth as he uttered a spell. In another second, my mind had become my own again, and I had returned to being a person. I held my breath as I tightened my hand around my wand, but I was too late. Silas whipped his wand through the water; my throat constricted, and I began to struggle to breathe. A hot jet of water pierced through the gloom and struck me in the chest. It was like a strong punch—my heart seized, and I careened deeper in the sea, the light turning to almost black.

I began to panic, struggling to swim toward the surface, but I was way too far down to get back to air. A streak of red raced toward me—Silas swimming toward me with full speed, his wand directed at me. My lungs opened to breathe as a bubble wrapped itself around my head. *What . . . why was he saving me?*

Silas swam closer to me now; he lifted his foot, and a hard boot connected with my chest, and I spiraled again.

"What are you doing?" I yelled, my voice taking on an ethereal tone through the bubble.

"Getting you back for the other day," he growled.

"Oh, shut up," I said, mentally calculating all the spells I knew in case I needed to use them. "Scion didn't hurt you too bad."

"Siphoners don't deserve to be at The Five Emergences," Silas spat.

"I'm *not* a siphoner just because y'all say my best friend was," I said.

"You need to leave the palace, and take your evil with you."

Before I could respond, Silas twirled his wand like a

sword fighter, sending multiple spells my way. I raised my own wand and counterattacked, dispelling as many as I could. We sparred in the water like we were fighting on earth, but I could never get the upper hand, could never go on offense. He sent all manner of spells my way, each of them more destructive than the last. A heavy pressure like the weight of a car slammed into me, and I lost consciousness for a second before I came back and counterattacked his next one, which sliced through the water like a battle-ax.

"Whoa," I breathed as a ball of swirling energy blasted toward me. My wand came up, dispelling it, and it exploded around me, its essence hot like lava. *How does he know so many spells?* I thought to myself.

Another spell left Silas's mouth. A force like a strong boot connected with my chest and then my leg. My wand dropped from my hand, and I heard a sickening *crunch* as the ribs in my chest broke. I gasped for breath in the bubble as I looked around for my wand.

"Not so tough without the bristlecone wand, huh?" Silas asked, right before he sent another spell my way. A crushing feeling hit my foot this time, and I gasped in pain, my stomach roiling from the agony. *Jaden, you have to do something.* But I couldn't do anything without my wand. Elijah's face bloomed in my mind as Silas smiled at me, the red of his aura striking against the deep blue of the sea.

I closed my eyes. *I can do this; I know I can. I just need to believe.*

I opened my eyes as his wand pointed at me again. I was done with Silas and his bullying. A fire built up inside me, like a burn coursing through my veins. My eyes narrowed as my hands came up, my fingers interlocking. When I opened them, a jet of flame burst from my chest, so bright that it was blinding.

A look of terror dawned in Silas's eyes as it connected with him. He screamed almost immediately. The fire consumed him to the point where I couldn't see him anymore; it burned through the water that surrounded us.

I stared at my hands while Silas screamed, my heart beating fast. "What did I do? I—I didn't mean to!"

A barrier of sorts slammed in between Silas and me, a see-through barrier that quivered when I reached out to touch it. With a jerk, an unseen force settled underneath me and Silas and lifted us upward, whipping through the water so fast that I could barely make out the screaming Silas on the other side of the obstruction. With a strong *push*, we were lifted out of the pool and settled on the concrete floors of the dungeon.

Professor Genesis ran over to us with her wand raised, every student crowding behind her.

"There is *no* fighting at The Five Emergences," she shrieked, engulfing the burning Silas with a dry chemical foam from her wand. When she was done, his eyes rolled to the back of his head, and he fell unconscious.

Everybody stared at me in horror, including Mikael and Scion. I didn't know what to do with my hands, what to do with what had just happened.

"*What* did you do?" Genesis said.

"I—I don't know," I said. "It just happened. He tried to attack me and . . ."

"Lies," Peter said from behind Genesis. "There's no way you could beat a fae without attacking him first. He's a siphoner, *just* like Elijah." Everyone murmured their agreement except for Mikael and Scion, but their terrified faces would live with me forever.

"He should be expelled! He doesn't deserve to be here!" Justice exclaimed.

Genesis pointed to Nahri and Erick. "Get him to the hospital." She glared at me, gazing at my broken foot and ribs. "Looks like you need some healing too." After Nahri and Erick picked up Silas and carried him out, she gestured to everyone after grabbing my cape, socks, and boots. "Class is over. Everyone has received a passing score. I'll take Jaden to the hospital.

"*You*," she said, taking me by the hand as everyone filed out of the dungeons.

"Look, I didn't—"

"I know," she said, helping me into the hallway as it cleared of students. "I'm not unaware of Silas's actions here. He thinks he owns this school because he's the fae heir." Her eyes turned stormy as she marched me through passageways I hadn't seen before, climbing up broad stairs.

"Then why did you act like it was my fault?" I said as I huffed, puffed, and limped behind her, holding on to my chest.

My injuries felt like someone had taken a baseball bat and treated my body like a punching bag.

"Because of Silas's parents," she said as she steered us to a closed door with a red cross on it. "I'd never hear the end of it if he told them I'd taken your side."

"And heaven forbid you take up for a person who believes that Elijah was good," I said, glowering at her.

"Listen," she said, staring at me as the sterile scent of the hospital tickled my nose. I thought I saw her eyes turn glassy, but when she blinked, the tears were gone. "I'll need to tell Carmine what happened, but I'll make sure that you're not expelled."

I decided to take her pity for me as a way to learn more about Elijah.

"You said in class that the transformation bracelets couldn't be taken off unless a professor gives permission," I blurted out. I kept going as her eyes narrowed. "I want to know how Elijah and Luxor disappeared if the bracelets track every Sorcerer who wears one."

She grabbed my arm again, but this time, her grip was soft. She leaned closer and whispered. "I can't speak for Luxor. But as for Elijah, a siphoner can do all manner of magic; they'd only have to leech the magic from the bracelet to release the spell on it. Another reason why the Ruin keeps growing."

I gulped, trying to process what she'd told me. "Okay."

"Now, let's get a nurse in the hospital ward to heal you."

When Genesis pushed the hospital door open, I glanced

around, noticing that the ward was empty, save for a bandaged Silas, who was already lying down in one of the beds. She sent a glare his way as she pushed me farther into the room, handing me my clothing. "Carmine will be here any second. I'll leave you now. Silas won't try to fight you since he's in no shape to."

"What about my wand? It fell in the pool."

She winked at me. "I'll retrieve it for you. And I'll tell your friends to come check in on you."

And with that, she turned on her heels and left.

My thoughts whirred as my mind came up with the next step of my plan.

I just needed to get Mikael and Scion to agree with it.

CHAPTER NINETEEN

A nurse was attending to me and Silas when Headmaster Carmine arrived, holding my wand. I had just gulped the medicinal healing tea the nurse had given me, and as I sat up from my bed, my ribs reset with a pleasurable *crunch*.

"I didn't do it!" I began to protest. "I mean, I did it, but I didn't do it. Does that even make sense?"

Carmine's eyes grew stormy. "Mr. Powers, no excuses. You need to take responsibility for your actions."

"But I didn't! It was Silas, he—"

"He *attacked* me," Silas yelled, springing awake as his burns healed. An IV stuck out from his arm. A shining light drifted from the attached bag and flowed into his body. He pushed the nurse away. "I can't believe he attacked me!"

My foot reset itself, and I grunted before getting out of the hospital bed, completely tired of the lies. "He attacked me first! And he's been doing it since I came here! All I did was respond! It's not fair that he gets to act like this school is his, just because of who he is and where he comes from. He's even accused me of being a siphoner!"

Carmine tossed Silas a furious glare. "Is this true?"

A dark growl emitted from Silas's throat as he got out of bed and lunged at me. "You liar—"

"Silas!" the nurse yelled.

Bang. Carmine swung his wand as I tensed for a fight. Silas fell to the floor midflight, his wand flying through the air to Carmine's outstretched hand.

Silas cowered in front of Carmine, unable to move further. Carmine tilted his head to the side, and the nurse left the room with a hurried gait.

"This is despicable!" Carmine said. "The way you're acting assures me that Mr. Powers is telling the truth, Silas. This place is not your playground, and Jaden is not your punching bag." Carmine sniffed. "But it looks like *you're* the real punching bag here." I stifled a laugh before Silas spoke again.

"But—"

"Silence!" Carmine yelled, sparks flying from his wand. "No more of your insolence." He tossed my wand back to me. "Apologize to each other and get back to class. I don't want to hear anything about you fighting anymore. You're Sorcerers— learn to act like it!" He shifted his gaze to me now. "I believe Professor Genesis's story of what happened. I know you're not

195

at fault here, but if you ever fight in my halls again, you're gone. Understood?"

"Yes, Headmaster."

"Can I have my wand back?" Silas grumbled.

Carmine kneeled to give it back, turned on his heels, and walked out of the hospital, slamming the door behind him.

The spell broke and Silas stood, adjusting his clothing. He made to leave too, but I needed to know more; if we were going to stop fighting, that would mean we needed to talk at least.

"Why do you hate me so much?" I asked the retreating Silas. "I mean, I'm Elijah's best friend, sure, but that's not enough."

Silas turned to me, his look so deadly that I would've been blown to pieces if it were magical. "Elijah was a menace. I heard that he came here acting like he was better than everyone just for him to turn evil."

"I'm not Elijah though," I said, taking a step toward him. "You can't blame me for being someone I'm not."

"You've beaten me twice," Silas said, sneering. "Seems to me that you're just like him."

While beating him should've given me a source of pride, it didn't. I'd never wanted to hurt him like this.

Silas approached me now, bumping his chest against mine. His voice lowered as he pointed to the bristlecone wand in my hand. "And you have that. A siphoner's best friend should *not* have a wand that even Carmine doesn't have. I don't know if you're truly like Elijah, but I know you don't belong here."

I pushed him away from me. "I do belong here, and I'll prove it to everyone someday."

Silas pushed me back, narrowing his eyes. "Keep thinking like that and you'll end up evil, just like Elijah."

"Listen, I didn't choose to get magic this way. It just happened to me. I can't help that the bristlecone wand bonded with me."

"What did you just say?" Silas whispered, pushing me against the wall behind me.

"I—I just meant that I had an Outburst just like everyone else. And that I can't control a wand bonding with me."

Silas snarled. "Stay away from me."

And with that, he walked out of the hospital, leaving me alone.

When Mikael and Scion came to get me from the hospital ward, my plan had crystallized, and I was ready to put it into action.

"I want to break into Professor Genesis's office," I announced, after telling them what had just happened.

"What?" Scion balked. "Why?"

"Genesis said that the bracelets track the location and time a Sorcerer uses a spell. That means that she might know where Elijah is, right? And maybe Luxor."

"But why would she know that and not tell Carmine?" Mikael asked. He pulled out the pad we'd worked on earlier with our list of suspects. "And we never added Genesis to the list. We're jumping all over the place! I'm confused!"

But Scion's eyes glowed with a curiosity that let me know that she was game. "She said she doesn't know the spell to take the bracelets off . . . but she didn't say that she didn't have the records of the bracelets' tracking. She's the Metamorphosis professor, so the safest place for those records to be is in her office."

I pointed an index finger at her, nodding. "Exactly!"

Mikael paced the ward. "Oh my . . . oh my . . . we're gonna get expelled if we do this. It's against the rules to break into a professor's office, especially after you just got in a fight with Silas!"

"A fight that I won," I said. "And Carmine didn't expel me. He yelled at us, yes, but that was it. He's not going to get rid of me; he needs me to figure out where Elijah is by going through my memories."

Mikael shivered. "Do you know what happens to a person if they break into a professor's office without them present? They put all types of curses on their offices!"

Scion snapped her fingers. "You just answered your question," she said, grinning. "Genesis is in her office. She said she was going back there when she sent me and Mikael to come get you. If she's in her office . . ."

"Then there's no curse," Mikael breathed.

I took the sleeping potion I'd won in Elixirs out of my pocket. "We can use this."

It was Scion's turn to gape at me. "Jaden!"

I shrugged. "She'll be asleep while we search and probably won't even remember we were in her office when she awakens. No harm, no foul."

Before they could say anything else, I was strolling out of the hospital ward and heading to the dungeons, but I stopped when Mikael put a hand on my shoulder, huffing loudly. "Her office is upstairs, remember?"

"Right," I said, turning around and heading toward her office. "Wait, that means you're going along with this plan?"

Scion rolled her eyes. "Listen, we both believe Elijah is innocent; if we're going to get expelled, we might as well do it together."

I breathed a sigh of relief as we stepped into Genesis's classroom and went to her office's open doorway. Inside, Genesis was muttering to herself, her back turned to us. An opening in the wall behind her desk was encircled with fire. A steaming cup of coffee sat on her desk, two miniature dragons blowing fire into it.

"That has to be where the records are kept," I whispered, nodding at the opening in the wall.

"Professor Genesis," Scion called.

She turned to us, her eyes confused, her wand gripped. "What are you three doing here?"

"You said in class that the transformation bracelets couldn't be taken off unless a professor gave permission," I blurted out. I kept going as her eyes narrowed. "I want to know how Elijah and Luxor disappeared if the bracelets track every Sorcerer who wears one."

She folded her arms. "I've already told you that Elijah could've siphoned the magic from his."

We stepped inside and walked closer to her desk, me hiding the sleeping potion behind my back.

"But that doesn't make—" I began.

"Listen," Genesis said, as she turned her back to us again, holding her wand aloft. She muttered a spell, and the circle of fire blazing around the wall began to close inch by inch. "Mr. Powers, I may have told you that I don't like Silas and his family either, but my patience is running thin with you today."

While she spoke, I moved fast and slipped a few drops of the potion into her coffee. The two dragons sent what looked like scathing looks to me and disappeared in clouds of smoke. Genesis turned around and gripped her coffee, sitting down at her desk. "I've already told you everything I know." She gestured to the closing opening behind her. "And only my wand and voice can access the bracelet records, so good luck with that."

Come on, come on, I mentally urged as Genesis drank from the cup and the circle of fire inched closed even more. *How long was this potion supposed to take to work?*

"Well, we just—" Scion began. Genesis's eyes widened, she grunted in surprise, and then fell asleep.

"Quick!" Mikael screamed. "Before the portal closes!"

We jumped through the circle of fire before it became too small. It bloomed open as we struggled.

We found ourselves in a walled-off room, filled with gray filing cabinets.

I glanced back at the sleeping Genesis. "How long is she supposed to be out?"

Scion glared at me. "You'd think you'd know that considering *you* won the sleeping potion!" she said with a sarcastic tone.

"Listen, let's just hurry, find what we need, and get outta here," Mikael said hurriedly.

With that, we took to opening each of the filing cabinets until I found a folder marked "Elijah Williams."

"Here," I said triumphantly, bringing it over to them. "We need to see this."

I opened the folder, holding my chest to catch my breath. Inside were reams and reams of pages, detailing the days and times Elijah used a spell. "Whoa, there have to be thousands of entries here! Jeez, he was so good!"

"What else?" Scion asked, her eyes full of wonder.

I continued to shuffle. "If these are in order by time and location, then that means"—I turned to the last page—"the last entry should correspond to when he disappeared."

And there it was, two entries. One entry stated, "Elijah Williams, palace Puddle, 6:00 p.m."

"That must be from right before Carmine placed Elijah under an enchanted sleep," I mused. "He said he saw Elijah coming out of a Puddle, drenched in blood."

"Keep reading," Mikael suggested.

The last entry stated, "Elijah Williams, palace entrance, bracelet removed, 9:00 p.m."

I gasped. "Wait . . . then that would mean . . ."

Scion nodded, catching on. "Mm-hmm."

"Carmine was right. Elijah woke up from the enchanted sleep and then disappeared. But that still doesn't answer the question of how he was able to take off his bracelet though," Mikael pointed out.

"Wait," I said, continuing to dig through the filing cabinets until I found another folder labeled "Nicholas Luxor." I shuffled through it until I came to his last entry, my heart feeling like it had stopped as I read aloud: "Nicholas Luxor, palace entrance, bracelet removed, nine p.m.

"Luxor," I breathed. "It *has* to be him that removed the bracelets. He *must* be holding Elijah captive somewhere! They're together! That's why Elijah sent me that message to help him!"

Behind us, Genesis groaned, beginning to stir a bit.

Scion hurriedly took the folders from me and placed them back inside the filing cabinets where we'd found them. "We should go."

And with that, we ran out of the office and classroom, my mind whirring with thoughts.

Is that why Elijah gave me his magic through Inheritance magic? Because Luxor was the one who was evil, who had caused the Ruin to appear, and not him? Was it because he knew that Luxor would drain him of the rest of his magic, so he gave me most of it to keep Luxor from getting it?

There were so many questions I still had, but the pieces of the puzzle were finally coming together.

CHAPTER TWENTY

More questions swirled around my mind as we went to the final new class scheduled for the day, Artwork. How *had* I done that to Silas? Carmine had said that Sorcerers could only do magic with their wands, so how did I hurt Silas without one? Could it have been my Inheritance magic? I needed to research in the library as soon as possible.

And . . . I couldn't keep it in anymore. I had to tell Scion and Mikael about my magic. That way, they could trust me. Plus, I was tired of being alone with this.

"Wait, where is Artwork? And what is Artwork?" I said aloud, looking down at my schedule. A word appeared next to the class name: "Spell." "Why does finding classes around here have to be so hard?" The hallways were empty now too, since the next class had already started.

"If Artwork needs to be found with a spell, then maybe we needed to cast a Locator spell to find it?" Scion suggested.

I took out my wand. "Chọta Artwork." A blue pulse emitted from the tip of my wand and hovered in front of us. As we stepped forward once, it moved forward. "Hmm." We kept walking, and it flew, guiding us down staircases and past doorways until we came to another empty hallway. In front of us, a huge, cloudy crystal ball floated in the air. The pulse disappeared as we approached it.

"Now that's dope," I said.

The crystal ball hummed, somehow beckoning us closer. When it engulfed us, we were lost to darkness and swirling shadows. A bright light surrounded us next, and then we stood in a misty classroom, a sweet scent wafting past our noses. Our first-year section was standing away from the desks that dotted the room. I guess we weren't too late.

The smoke in the room gathered in a hazy cloud, and a tall person appeared. The fog dispersed through the rest of the class as they stepped forward, a top hat settled on their head.

"Lathan Achilles," he said, wrapping his cloak around him for dramatic effect. "Welcome to Artwork." No one really knew what to say to that.

Gorgona raised her hand. "What's Artwork?"

Achilles smiled, his dark hair falling into his yellow eyes as he winked. "Sit down and I shall tell you." Scion and Mikael both gave me a small smile as we found desks near one another.

"Artwork is a fancy name that I've given to Prophecy," Achilles began, swirling around in clouds of smoke. He appeared and disappeared in multiple places around the room as he circled us. "Divining is the act of seeing into the past, present, and future. However, crystal balls are so old school."

He swept his wand around the classroom, and our desks filled with markers, pencils, colored pencils, paper, erasers, and paint. An easel appeared next to each of our workstations.

Several whoops of excitement filled the room, except from me. Just like I didn't know how to cook, I definitely didn't know how to draw. But I did know what I wanted to see.

"The past and present are set in stone," Achilles continued. "But the future is open, so you must use care in divining it. Every action has a reaction; every cause has an effect. Which means, every decision you make creates a different future."

He pointed his wand near the middle of the room, and white lights discharged from the tip, forming a straight line. "This is us, in linear form. This is our current present and past." Two lights in the middle floated above the others and formed a branch on the top and the bottom. "A different future bursts forth when a choice is made. A different branch. Divining the future is hard because every choice affects everything."

Mikael raised his hand. "So, what's the point, then? If the future is not set in stone, why practice"—he gestured at his workstation—"Artwork?"

Achilles swirled in smoke and appeared next to Mikael, who yelped in surprise. "Because the future gives you suggestions on how to proceed. It gives you multiple checkpoints and pathways to making a decision."

Achilles circled around the room again before appearing at the front of the class. "I would advise you all to stick to the past and the present. Many diviners have become so infatuated with the future that they get lost in it." He cleared his throat. "And by lost, I mean *really* lost. They don't exist in the present anymore." Every student tensed at that.

"We should start!" Achilles smiled, like he hadn't just scared us. He taught us the spell to use and then swept around the room, giving pointers as we worked. He helped me position my wand over my paper—since I had already decided not to paint anything on the easel—and coached me through.

"To cast your spell, think about what or who you want to see, and then let the spell do its work," he whispered as I gripped my wand, pointing its tip down vertically.

"I'm ready," I said. He nodded and disappeared in a cloud of fog.

I cleared my mind. "Gosi m ihe mere mgbe gara aga." There was no spark of light, but the air grew heavier than it already was and my eyes closed, my hand moving automatically across the white construction paper with my pencil. *Show me Elijah. Show me what happened to him.* When I opened my eyes, I had drawn two rudimentary stick figures, one to represent Elijah and the other for Professor Luxor. And that wasn't all. Everything disappeared around me, except for that gray haze that permeated everything. But just like when Carmine studied me, I felt no fear, no terror. It just *was*.

There was comfort in that silence.

The figures twitched a bit on the page, then lifted off, standing in front of me at full attention as I gasped. The Elijah figure reached a hand to me, his voice speaking through the line lip.

"Do you want to see?" it said.

"Elijah?"

"Not Elijah, per se, but close enough to him. I can show you the past like you requested. Do you want to see?"

"Yes."

Elijah inclined his head to the Luxor figure who blinked once, and then they both disappeared. The gloom dissipated next, and I found myself in the real world, but still rooted to my desk.

One of the grand courtyards of The Five Emergences rose around me, large statues of the first professors located at each point of the square. My heart hitched when I saw Elijah, standing across from Luxor. He didn't look like the Elijah I was used to. He seemed taller here with his wand held at his side; his hair flowed down his back in enchanted burgundy locs, the cape twirling around him the color of forest green.

Luxor mumbled a few words, and wisps of smoke emerged from his wand, flowing around the space. "There. No one should be able to hear our conversation. What did you want to talk with me about?"

"Professor," Elijah began in an incredibly soft voice as he took a step forward. Before he could speak again, his knees folded underneath him and he fell toward the ground. Luxor caught him in his arms and settled him against one of the statues. He took a step back and watched Elijah, whose face was now drowning with sweat.

"Elijah, what have you gotten yourself into?" Luxor commanded, disappointment burning in his tone. "I know we've been studying all types of magic together, but I don't recognize this."

"It's not me," Elijah managed to say before digging into his pocket, pulling out a piece of parchment, and handing it over to Luxor. "I've been noticing this for a while. You know I practice magic all the time. But, I'm afraid . . ."

Elijah took out a handkerchief and blotted the sweat from his face.

"Afraid of what?" Luxor asked.

Elijah shook his head as Luxor read, horror dawning on his face as he did.

"You . . . you can't mean . . . ?"

"I don't think it's a coincidence that I was four years old when I had my Outburst," Elijah began. "Magic has been trying to tell us something ever since then. I've excelled in every form of magic like no young child is supposed to. But, now, every time I cast magic, I find myself getting weak. I feel magic literally leaking out of me, out of my body. Someone here is siphoning magic, Professor Luxor. And I believe they are coming for me first because I'm the most powerful kid here."

"What?" Luxor said, flabbergasted, holding out the parchment. "This is your research? How can this be true? Every time I practice magic, I feel fine!"

Elijah leaned forward. "Listen to what I'm saying, please! I had my Outburst at age four."

Luxor was quiet for a while as he closed his eyes and thought. "Oh . . . Outbursts are uncontrollable bouts of magic, some of the most powerful magic there is."

"In children," Elijah finished, disgust clouding his speech. "Someone is siphoning magic from *children*. And I bet other students have noticed, but I'm the first one to put everything together."

Luxor opened his eyes and pulled out his wand. The parchment burst into flames. "We'll need to keep this to ourselves for now," he warned. "And do some investigating." He patted Elijah on the shoulder. "I guarantee you that if you've noticed that someone is siphoning magic, then that means that the culprit *knows* that you know too. They could try to magically control you."

Elijah shuddered. "I'll do what I can to protect myself, Professor."

"If someone is siphoning magic from the children of Wonder, Mr. Williams . . ."

"Then the world as we know it could end," Elijah finished.

The image disappeared, leaving me in total gray.

"That's it?" I asked. "I need to see what happened to my friend! Where is Elijah?"

"That's all. The record ends there," Elijah's stick figure said, reappearing in the gloom.

"What does that even mean?" I asked.

"It means that a spell is at work, probably," Elijah said. "Whoever cast it knew that someone would probably try to look into their past or present."

"That could only mean . . . ," I began.

The stick figures disappeared then, and the hazy smoke of the classroom returned. Achilles stood in the front, checking his watch. Everyone seemed to be in a trance as they drew, colored, or painted. My pencil was still in my hand. Drool ran from Scion's mouth as she scribbled on her paper.

Achilles clapped his hands. "Two hours have passed, children. Class is now over."

"Whoa," Mikael said, his trance broken. "That didn't even seem like that long!"

I stretched to the sky, disturbed at what I had seen. I glanced at Mikael and Scion as everyone packed their belongings and began to file out of the classroom.

"We need to talk," I said. "I have a lot to tell you."

I was convinced now.

It was Luxor.

Elijah found out someone had been siphoning magic and told his mentor, not knowing that Luxor was the culprit. I was convinced now too, that Carmine saying he saw Elijah with a wild look in his eyes right before he disappeared was just Luxor casting a spell on him, just like he had told Elijah someone would do.

I was done hiding. I needed my friends' help, and the only way they'd really trust me was if I told them the full truth.

Elijah's life might depend on it.

CHAPTER TWENTY-ONE

That night at dinner, an announcement from Carmine delayed my confessions, but also confirmed my decision to be honest with my friends.

Midway through our meal, a smoky screen bloomed in the middle of the cafeteria causing all the students to jump out of their seats. The smoke dissipated, and Carmine appeared, clearing his throat before he spoke.

"I'm devastated to report that the Ruin has attacked a treasured monument in our community."

Every student gasped, shouts ringing out in the space. Carmine held his hands upward as the screen split into two. "Silence, children."

We grew quiet as the right side of the screen flickered on, showing an aerial view of an inviting building that sat on top of a familiar-looking mountain.

"That's Matthias's Wandshop!" I whispered.

"Shh," Scion whispered. "I wanna hear this."

Carmine was silent as the Ruin appeared in the sky to the left of the wandshop. It was a deep, black hole of swirling electrical energy, so imposing that it made every student catch their breaths. It careened downward with a *boom*, falling and crashing into the wandshop's ceiling. The entire left side of the building exploded in flames. I couldn't help but yelp as I remembered the first time I'd seen the Ruin.

"It's grown," I said.

As if it could hear me, the Ruin grew even bigger, and a ravenous moan emitted from it as it ate up the building's magic.

Matthias ran out of the building, holding her wand aloft, expelling protective spells. As quickly as it had appeared, the Ruin disappeared in a blink of an eye. The clip looped and played again as Carmine spoke.

"The Ruin grows as it eats magic. The protective spells surrounding the wandshop were not strong enough to withstand it. I assure you, though, that we are doing the best we can to experiment with magic to cast more powerful spells against it."

"What about The Five Emergences?" I whispered to Scion. "Will it be protected?"

"As far as our school," Carmine continued, "the Ruin has no place here. With me in power, it will not do any damage to us. Some parents have already inquired about ending the school year early, but I have assured them that you will be safe here. And I intend to keep that promise. Finish your dinner and be careful in your studies. We will repair the wandshop and return normalcy to our worlds."

He paused and cleared his throat again. "And to Elijah Williams. We will find you. And we will cast the siphoning magic from your blood and bring the Ruin to heel. If anyone knows of his whereabouts, please don't hesitate to let us know. Entire worlds depend on it."

Every eye turned to me as the screen winked out of existence.

I shifted uncomfortably in my seat, turning to my friends to stop everyone from staring at me. "Let's go to the library. We need to research. And I need to tell you the truth."

We climbed the staircase of the tallest tower to the library. My heart beat faster and faster as we reached the entrance.

I was going to tell them my deepest secret. What if they didn't accept me?

"I have something to admit," I began as Mikael pushed the doors open. "I don't know how you're gonna feel about it. But something happened when I was in the pool with Silas. And I think it's connected to why I'm here, why Carmine wants to study me, and possibly to Elijah." My mind had been whirring with possibilities ever since we had left Artwork, and I needed to put them into words.

"Let's just go inside first," I said. "And then I can tell you everything."

Scion cast a Silence enchantment as we entered so no one—and especially not Silas—could hear what we were talking about. The library was dim, but one of the biggest and most magical things I had ever seen. Bookshelves rose from the floor, towering high in what looked like an open sky, rising into the air as far as the eye could see. Unseen energies pushed books into their assigned slots, took them out and reshelved them—the books released contented sighs when set in their preferred places—and dusted the inside and outside of them. An enormous book the size of a human was fixed in place on the floor, an invisible energy flipping its golden pages.

Librarians—most of them not human—shuffled among the bookshelves carrying wands. A vampire librarian strolled down an aisle with a bored look on her face. She whipped her wand lazily in the air, making books fly across the library to a counter where another librarian checked their serial numbers and placed them in a stack labeled "checked out."

We walked past a section where books sat on their shelves bragging to one another in hushed tones.

"My pages contain the secrets of unicorn magic," a dusty black book said, its pages frayed.

"Well, *I* just got here," another book boasted, shining with newness. "I was created by a great Sorcerer, on the different properties of love potions."

"I wish you *all* would shut up," an elven librarian muttered as he dusted off their spines. "Every time I come over here, you're always arguing. Go to sleep. Please!"

"Let's find somewhere quiet," Mikael said, stepping into

another section of the library that consisted of small, comfy-looking rooms with couches, beanbags, desks, and lamps that emitted soft white light.

"How do we get books here?" I said, staring into space at the towering bookshelves. Huge stacks of books were just piled on top of one another, fixed together by some magical force. "If you touch one book, won't the entire place fall down?"

Scion pulled me into a room where she pointed at a gigantic tome set on the desk. "It would be impossible to know what you're looking for here," she said. "You'll have to look through this catalogue, point your wand at the title you want, and then a librarian will bring it to you to either look through or check out."

We all sat around the catalogue, and I told them the full truth of what happened in the pool with Silas.

Scion's eyes widened. "You can't use your magic without a wand!"

"That's what everyone says," I said. "But I promise you, I did *not* use my wand when Silas attacked me." I pointed at my chest. "It came from inside of me, like a living thing. It some-how knew I was in a bad situation, and it just . . . saved me, I guess." I shrugged while Mikael just stared at me in awe.

"I wonder what it all means," Scion said. "Do you think it has anything to do with Elijah?"

I took a deep breath. It was time to reveal my biggest secret. They'd either continue to be my best friends or they'd tell everybody what they knew, and I'd be cast out of magic school. "I believe it has everything to do with him and why I'm here."

"What does that mean?" Scion asked.

I took another breath and told them about the vision I'd had in Artwork regarding Elijah realizing that someone at the school was siphoning magic and what Carmine had found out about me.

"I believe the way I got magic is the reason I was able to beat Silas in the pool, and probably why the bristlecone wand bonded with me. I think Elijah gave me magic, somehow. Carmine called it Inheritance magic," I ended.

They were silent for a while.

"Wait, *what*?" Mikael said.

"Inheritance magic is . . . something that almost never happens in our world," Scion whispered. She took out her wand and cast another Silence enchantment. "You can*not* let anyone in this building hear you say that!"

"Are you sure?" Mikael said. "Is Carmine sure?"

They hadn't run away from me yet, but they both looked like they wanted to bolt any second now if I didn't give them the full story. "Carmine didn't even need to tell me because . . . I had my Outburst literally a day before I came here." I took out Elijah's notebook while they gasped in shock. "And it was after I read this. I fainted in his bedroom, woke up, and caused my parents' car to crash."

"And you're just telling us this *now*?" Scion shrieked.

"Carmine told me not to tell anyone," I said. "I didn't know what else to do. But I'm tired of keeping this secret. I believe that I have this magic for a reason. I have no magical ancestry or ties to this world, not like you two. And I believe that Elijah gave me this magic so that I could come to The Five Emergences and find him."

I paused again as I weighed their reaction. Their mouths hung open like yawning doors as they sent each other wordless glances.

"Jaden, Inheritance magic is... powerful magic that nobody really understands," Mikael said. "Wow! Who would've thought I would be best friends with Jaden Powers, a powerful Sorcerer and the best friend of another amazing Sorcerer, Elijah?"

"You're right, we need to do some research," Scion said, standing and opening the huge tome. "We need to figure out if there is any information on Inheritance magic in here, how to use it, and the connection it gives you to Elijah."

"Wait, so y'all aren't mad at me? Like, you're not gonna stop being my friends?"

Scion rolled her eyes as she scanned the index. "No, I'm not. Just because I don't understand you doesn't mean I hate you. That's the problem with Silas and the fae; they think that they should be able to dominate other supernatural creatures because they don't understand them, and that's not true."

Mikael grabbed my shoulder. "And you know I'm not going anywhere."

My heart swelled with happiness as I stood next to Scion to help her scan. All this time I was scared they wouldn't accept me, when I had been missing that they were special too.

"What are we looking for?" I asked. "And why is this book so huge?"

"It contains all of the information about magic in the known world," Scion said, taking her hand and scrolling through the A section.

"And the *unknown* world," Mikael said, shivering.

"If Inheritance magic is so unknown, then maybe we should look somewhere else," I suggested. "It wouldn't just be in the index all out in the open, right?"

Mikael scanned the page until he pointed to a section labeled "Forbidden—Or Is It?" "Well, that's *not* ominous."

"Good idea," Scion said, pointing her wand at it.

"Who is disturbing me?" a voice said.

We all jumped back. "What was that?" I asked.

"No clue," Mikael whispered.

"It's me, duh," the voice continued. "Look down at the index."

When we did, a ghostly figure crawled out of the tome in the space next to the "Forbidden" label and plopped down in front of us. I screamed once, then clapped my hand over my mouth. The Five Emergences was no longer scary to me, but I wasn't used to ghosts jumping out of ancient indexes.

The ghost was dressed in old-looking clothes, complete with a topcoat, cane, low-heeled leather shoes with buckles, and a tricorn hat, which he took off before bowing to us. "Professor Uniscus Washington at your service, ghost and procurer of the 'Forbidden—Or Is It?' section of the library index."

"You're dead?" I asked.

"Jaden!" Scion said, gasping.

"That's quite all right," Uniscus said. "I mean, I am dead. No need to sugarcoat it."

"Can you help us?" I asked.

"Depends on what it is."

"Inheritance magic," Mikael said. "We need to know everything this library has about it."

An image of a book appeared in Uniscus's ghostly head, flipping faster and faster through uncountable pages. "I'm afraid there's only one book with a reference to that," Uniscus said. "And it's not in this library. It's in the White Witch's library thousands of miles away from here."

"Wait, the White Witch from Narnia exists?" I asked. "I remember reading about her when I was younger."

"Darn it," Scion groaned. "I guess we can't see that book."

Uniscus *hmphed*, obviously offended. "Just because it's not here doesn't mean that I can't get it. Who do you take me for? Now, do you want it or not?"

I hurriedly nodded. "Yes, please."

With an annoyed grumble, Uniscus dove back headfirst into the index, and we could hear the distinct sounds of glass breaking, a cat screeching, and water splashing.

We glanced at one another.

Uniscus appeared again after a few minutes, jumping out of the tome, carrying a worn black book in his hand. "I've found the book you wanted. *Obscure Magic*, it is called. It wasn't easy getting it."

"What happened?" Scion asked.

"Let's just say . . . Jadis, the White Witch, isn't an easy person to talk to." He handed the book over to me. "Is that all?"

"Thank you, Uniscus."

"Glad to be of service," he said, tipping his hat to us and jumping back into the index.

Scion pushed the index to the side while I set the book on the desk with trembling fingers. "This will give us the answers I've been looking for," I whispered. "I don't know if I'm ready."

A warm hand grabbed mine and squeezed. "This could lead us to Elijah," Mikael said.

After taking a deep breath, I opened the book. It felt like it was *guiding* me, reacting to the magic in my blood. "Whoa," I said as my hands rose above the pages; they flipped on their own accord, a bright light shining from their depths. It was *good*, almost like whatever was inside me was finding its place back home. Like it had been trying to tell me this from the beginning. How weird.

"You don't see that every day," Scion remarked.

The pages settled on a blank page in the middle, and words scrawled on it in a cursive script, black and bold.

Welcome Intrepid Reader,

Only those with Obscure magic in their blood can access these pages. And we have detected it within you. Would you like to proceed? Press your wand to this page if "yes." If "no," close this book and return it to where you found it.

I pressed my wand to the page, and it flipped to the next one, that same script writing across the parchment.

Obscure magic can be classified as the Sixth Emergence, but slim research has been done into the topic. It has no structure, shows no evidence, and has popped up randomly throughout the centuries.

There are four categories of Obscure magic: Love, Prophecy, Interdimensional, and Fundamental.

Love magic consists of births, deaths/transition, and romance between two or more beings. It is said that King Arthur and Guinevere shared a love between them that caused mountains to crumble, seas to thrash, and armies to be conquered.

Prophecy magic differs from divining in that it does not call for the practitioner to use an orb, drawings, or etchings for answers, and it can predict the future in precise and specific terms. Nostradamus is a perfect example of this, and no greater has been seen since.

Interdimensional magic allows the user to travel between dimensions other than Earth and the Puddles; the last practitioner of Interdimensional magic would often bring objects between dimensions as evidence of her power, but she disappeared five hundred years ago. Information on her has been lost to history.

The last category, Fundamental magic, exists in the unexplainable, causing the Sorcerer to do powerful feats of magic through the force of their will. No official record exists of a Sorcerer who has been able to use Fundamental magic, but there have been rumors throughout the centuries of Sorcerers inheriting it from other Sorcerers.

We grew silent after reading.

"I've been able to do some incredible things, things even Elijah couldn't do. I defeated Silas in the metamorphosis pool without a wand, and"—I paused for a beat, whipping out my wand—"the bristlecone wand chose me, after being dormant for a thousand years. All of this can't be a coincidence. Inheritance magic falls in the last category."

"But you *inherited* magic, right?" Scion asked, scrunching her eyebrows. "You inherited it through . . . *what*? I mean, it's right there in the name."

I picked up Elijah's notebook and shuffled to the loose page with the plea for help. "There," I said, pointing downward at the dried splotches. "The ink is blotted. I cried when I was in his bedroom. I was feeling so empty and without answers and mad that no one was listening to me. It felt like the end of my world. When I cried . . . the tears fell on the page, causing the words here to translate and for me to faint. After I woke up, I got the invitation when I got home, and Carmine came to bring me here."

"Magic sometimes needs an anchor to hold it," Scion mused aloud. "A spell that big . . ." She paced around the room now, mumbling to herself.

"Spit it out!" Mikael said.

"Yes, you inherited magic from Elijah, but he didn't give it to you physically, because he wasn't there. When you cried on the page, the tears became the anchor for the spell. So, your *love* for him allowed Inheritance magic to take hold within you." She looked at me with admiration, the same way Carmine had when he realized that I had Inheritance magic. "You inherited magic, yes, but it was *created* by love too. That's two kinds of Obscure magic. Wow, you really are powerful! Makes sense why you were able to beat Silas in that pool."

Tears sprang to my eyes. "I do love him. So much. Y'all don't know how much I do."

Both hugged me now, so tight that it felt like we had become one, even if it was just for a few seconds.

"Oh, Jaden, I'm so sorry you had to go to your best friend's memorial," Scion said.

"And I'm so sorry you felt so alone," Mikael said. "I'm here for you. We both are."

"It was horrible, but I got magic out of it. And I know that I have it for a reason, because of my love for my friend. Maybe it's not as complicated as I thought or Carmine thought; I'm here because my tears activated the magic in Elijah's written words, somehow. My tears represented my love."

"That's so beautiful," Scion said.

"You inherited Elijah's magic through your tears," Mikael mused. "Based on the love you have for your friend."

Scion snapped her fingers. "Wait! Remember what we've

been learning in Magical Theory? Magic doesn't just happen; it has a mind of its own and can act of its own accord when it decides to."

I nodded in agreement, but then sighed. "That still doesn't explain what I'm supposed to do with this Inheritance magic. What's my purpose? We can speculate, but that's not evidence."

"Don't you see?" Scion asked. "The vision in Artwork gave you the answers."

"Luxor," I said, fully convinced now. "Elijah told him that he was scared that someone was siphoning magic from children."

"And Luxor told him to be careful," Mikael said.

"It's Luxor. That's why when Carmine saw Elijah that last time, Elijah looked possessed. Luxor must be controlling him through a spell and siphoning his magic. It's why Elijah reached out to me to save him," I said.

"Exactly. We have to find Luxor and stop him," Scion said.

"Uniscus," I called, shutting the black book and handing it back to him when he jumped out of the index. "Make sure you put this somewhere only *you* can find it."

He winked. "Oh, I will."

"I'm not sure why, but a part of me thinks that *no one* but us should have access to it in the future."

CHAPTER TWENTY-TWO

Before we knew it, November had come. For me, it was all a whirlwind. Not only was I studying harder than I ever thought possible; I was also dealing with all the knowledge we had learned about my Inheritance magic. It was a bit overwhelming, but I was proud that I had at least managed to earn passing grades in every class so far. Going to magic school was harder than going to regular, public school, but I wanted to *be* better here.

Because Elijah's life depended on my succeeding.

Plus, it was always good to see Silas sulking in the hallway with his friends every time he saw me.

One morning after I had enchanted three red stripes on the side of my hair, I started to go down the first-year staircase when my schedule burned in my pocket. I pulled it out to look at it and could see another class joining the others, rising from the bottom of the parchment in a bubble. "Creative Arts" was the name, and a notation was written on the side of it—"last new class of the year for first-years."

"Why would they give us a brand-new class now?" I grumbled.

"I heard Creative Arts was the best class here," Scion said, stepping out of her dorm hallway and joining me. We walked down the steps together. "Where's Mikael?"

"He went to eat early," I said.

"Any new updates?"

I shook my head. "None. Carmine hasn't called me in for a study session in weeks. And he won't give me updates on how the search is going."

"You'd think since he was invading your mind like a crumb snatcher he'd at least tell you what he found," Scion said.

"Yeah. Where's this new class anyway?"

Scion pointed at my schedule as we passed by the cafeteria where Mikael joined us. "What's that?"

What looked like a bird covered in fire flew all around the schedule and then burst into a puff of smoke as we approached our section of first-years on the first floor. *Screech.* The large window near the entrance of the palace burst open, sending glass flying everywhere. Justice and Peter dove out of the way, and we all screamed as a firebird the size of an elephant flew through the opening, its talons leaving a huge depression in the marble floor. Red, flaming feathers fell as a large man stood on its back.

"What the—" Mikael said.

"Professor Zayd Tristian," he said, taking a bow. We just stared at him.

He waved us over. "Well, what are you waiting for? Climb on the beast's back. It won't hurt you!"

I shrugged and smiled at Scion and Mikael. "Well?"

With more effort than I thought possible, the entire class climbed on top of the firebird. It only screeched once when Peter stepped on its wings. He stumbled backward and burst into flames when he hit the floor.

Tristian held out his hand. "You'd think a boy made of fire wouldn't be so fearful of another being made of fire."

Peter shot him a dirty look, but took his hand while the rest of the class laughed. I made a point to laugh even louder than everyone else; hey, it wasn't every day you got to laugh at the person who bullied you.

With a heavy *push* the firebird reared back—that cut off my laughter—and blasted through the window and out into the open air.

Mikael grabbed my hand. "Firebirds don't exist in our world!" he screamed.

I patted his hand. "It's okay, Mikael."

We soared over the palace three times, leaving trails of flame and smoke in our wake until Tristian set us down in a courtyard filled with workstations. We followed him off the firebird's back, all dazed and confused. Tristian waved his wand once, and it disappeared in a cloud of smoke as he stepped in front of us.

"Welcome to Creative Arts!" Everyone, besides Peter, clapped.

"Can I get one of those things?" Justice asked.

"First, sit at your workstations, and I'll explain the Creative Arts to you," Tristian said. We all scattered, Scion and Mikael and me taking a seat near one another. With a pleased huff, Tristian took off his hat, and long blond hair fell down his back. He paced in front of us, his purple cape flowing in the wind.

"What you saw looked like an act of metamorphosis, but can anyone explain why it was not true metamorphosis?"

"Firebirds don't exist in our world!" Mikael repeated, calling from his desk.

Tristian pointed at Mikael. "Exactly! They are considered mythological. But, the Creative Arts allows you to create whatever you want." He stared at us intently with piercing blue eyes. "*Whatever* you want."

"How did you create it?" Justice asked.

"Simple. Energy," Tristian said, continuing to pace. "Energy exists within this entire world, and every creature is made of it. Living energy." When he snapped his fingers, it was like a bomb had gone off. "And all living energy can be snuffed out."

We all grew quiet.

"The Creative Arts is the hardest magic to cast because you must create from the energy around you."

"That sounds cool," Mikael said.

Tristian sent Mikael a glare so icy that even I grew scared. "It's not *cool*. It's necessary at times, yes, but it's not cool. Most

Sorcerers don't use it." He paused for a second before continuing. "To use the Creative Arts, there is a high cost. This type of magic has consequences. To create something new, you must take from the living. There must be a give-and-take. For something new to live, you must greet death on another."

A terrified silence seized the entire class, and I was sure everyone could hear my heart beating fast in my chest. *Why are we learning this?*

"There is only one spell you need to know for this class," Tristian said, waving his wand. Jars appeared on each of our workstations, live beetles crawling around in them. "And yes, I know that this is an unpleasant realization for almost all of you, but I guarantee you that there is no other choice. As you've no doubt learned in Deterring Danger, not everyone and everything is out for your highest good. You'll need to defend yourself, yes, but there might come a time where you need the Creative Arts to—dare I say it?—get *creative.*"

He taught us the spell now, but I was so horrified that I didn't repeat it when everyone else did.

"You will create your own firebird using the beetles in your jars," Tristian explained. "And you have the entire class period. You may get started."

He walked in between our workstations as we worked. We all unscrewed the tops of our jars, but nobody really made a move to conjure our firebirds just yet. Not when something had to die in the process.

"Not so easy, is it?" Tristian asked when he came to me.

"I—I don't think I can do this," I responded.

He cocked a blond eyebrow. "What will happen when you need it in the future?"

"I won't need it," I said, my mind mentally riffling through my dreambook and textbooks. "I—I can just use metamorphosis or something if I need to."

"What if you're ensnared by a Sorcerer and he casts a curse that renders your magic obsolete?" Tristian asked, his mouth lengthening into a frown. "You won't be able to fight back or dispel their magic."

"Then the Creative Arts are something I can't use anyway," I mused as his frown deepened. "Right?"

"That's why the Creative Arts are important," Tristian continued. "It's the only type of magic you can use in that type of situation. Magic from outside of this world doesn't affect the rules of magic in this world."

"I can just cast a shield beforehand," I suggested.

Tristian shook his head. "If you have to cast a shield while going against a powerful Sorcerer, you've already lost."

"I really don't wanna do this."

I thought I could see pity flicker through Tristian's eyes. "You don't have to. But it might be the difference between survival and . . . something worse."

He walked away now, checking in with other students. A cry of surprise sounded in my ears, and a feeling of heat tickled the hair on my arms, but I ignored them because I knew a firebird had been made, and a beetle had died.

I concentrated on the jar, lifting a struggling beetle out of it and settling it on my workstation with my trembling wand pointed at it. *I really don't want to do this. I really, really don't want to do this.* But Tristian was right; if I was going to find Elijah, I would have to know enough magic to save myself if I ever needed to. I had been at magic school for almost three months, and Silas and his friends had already taught me that everything was on the table when it came to finding Elijah. I wasn't ignorant enough to believe that everything would always be roses and butterflies.

An image of a firebird bloomed in my mind as I continued to point my wand at the beetle. "Meputa." A surge of energy beat against my chest, and my wand vibrated as I felt invisible air emit from the tip. The beetle twitched once, and then died. Its energy rose from its body, tinged in bright blue. It stretched in the air, and a screech broke through the silence, a firebird appearing in the blue. It screeched again, its eyes finding mine. With a flourish, it settled on my shoulders, drowning in flame that did not burn.

I petted its head and looked around me, a feeling of triumph flooding my senses. Everyone in class had conjured their own firebird as well, some of them small, some of them as large as mine, but none as big as Tristian's. It felt like a push and pull, the way I connected with my firebird. Everywhere I looked, I could feel it scanning as well. When I stood, it rose to attention, and when I mentally commanded it to fly, it did so.

Showers of flame fell from the sky as the firebirds lifted into the air and flew around one another. It was beautiful at first as Tristian ran around the courtyard, laughing to his heart's content. Some, though, puffed out into plumes of smoke, disappearing completely. Peter groaned in despair when his disappeared, and Justice stamped his feet in annoyance when his flew over the ramparts of the palace and then burst so loud you would've thought a bomb had exploded.

"Excellent job, everyone!" Tristian yelled.

Mine screeched once more before I called it back to my shoulder.

Tristian walked around the courtyard as class ended, clipboard in hand, examining our firebirds. He handed each of us a slip of paper as he walked by. Peter groaned again, and my eyes noticed the grade: average. Justice yelled at Tristian as he passed by, "This is so unfair! I didn't mean to make it explode!"

"You could've hurt someone," Tristian said to him as he stepped to Scion. "Hmm," he said, examining her firebird. I hadn't noticed that Scion's was small, like a hummingbird, and seemed sickly with its gray fur. "What happened here?"

Scion puffed out her chest and pointed toward a brown piece of dead grass. "I couldn't kill the beetle. Fae Sorcerers have killed my people for centuries; I'm not adding to that kind of violence." Tristian sniffed once, nodded, and handed her a paper with the words "below average" on it.

"I admire and respect your empathy, but that won't help you in a dire situation."

He strolled over to Mikael whose firebird was still zipping around the courtyard, screams filling the air. It reminded me of Mikael, who couldn't be quiet if his life depended on it. "Average," Tristian said, handing him his slip. He must've noticed what I had. "Your created art should never be an extension of your personality, only of your mind."

Mikael huffed as Tristian came over to me.

"Perfect work," Tristian said, admiring my firebird. "You can extinguish it now."

I mentally *pulled*, and the firebird vanished into smoke as Tristian handed me a slip, which I read aloud. "Below average? Are you serious? That's almost a fail!"

"Almost!" Tristan said, snapping his fingers.

"You just said it was a perfect cast!"

"But you hesitated," Tristian responded, eyeing me with his steely gaze. "And Sorcerers can't hesitate, not when their lives are in danger."

I grumbled, "This isn't fair," as Tristian dismissed the class.

Scion, Mikael, and I trudged back to the palace on our own as the students dispersed.

"He's *not* a nice professor," Mikael said.

"He started off that way," I said, crumpling the almost failing grade in my hand.

"How can you do everything right and still get a bad grade?" Mikael said.

"Welcome to my world," Scion and I said at the same time. We looked at each other, laughed a bit, and continued to the palace. It felt good to provide some type of humor in our terror.

Thud. A lump appeared in my pants pocket as we stepped inside. I checked it and saw a note from Carmine, requesting another meeting with him. But it was dated for a time thirty minutes ago.

"Why am I just getting this now?" I asked, showing it to Mikael and Scion.

Scion shrugged. "Maybe the Creative Arts interfered with the magic, somehow?"

"Yeah, maybe." I paused for a moment. "I have to go," I said, running up the first-year staircase ahead of Mikael and Scion. "Maybe Carmine finally has an answer for where Elijah could be?"

They answered my question, but I was already too far away to hear it. The only thing that mattered was Elijah. And me telling Carmine what I'd learned about my magic with my friends. Once I got to Carmine's office, though, an icy conversation between two people emanated from his closed door.

"You were friends with Luxor, were you not? I've seen the pictures on your desk, Cayman." It was Carmine. His voice was usually soft, but authoritative. But this was different. A shiver rippled down my spine at his words—he sounded terrifying. I mean, he was always intimidating, but not like this.

"Yes, I was," Cayman responded, his voice timid at first, but growing more confident. "I mean, I *am* friends with him."

"Are you helping to hide it, Cayman? You know I need . . ."

Cayman gasped. "I would never, Headmaster. The Ruin is—"

"You do as I tell you; find the weapon, disarm it, or you're gone!"

What weapon are they talking about? Elijah?

"I'll do as you say."

The door opened then, and Cayman reared back as he noticed me standing there.

"Mr. Powers." Cayman nodded before marching off.

"Ah, Jaden," Carmine said from his desk, a bright smile on his face. "I see you've finally received my note. I should've known that if you were in Professor Tristian's class, he wouldn't allow any messages to infiltrate his lessons."

"I'm sorry I'm late," I said, entering the office.

"Nonsense," he said, pointing at the chair in front of his desk. "Are you ready to continue?"

I shifted from foot to foot. "Oh. I was kinda hoping that you had some answers by now."

Carmine shook his head. "Sadly, still nothing. We must keep working."

I sat, while debating if I should tell Carmine about the book on Obscure magic. But what about what I had just heard between him and Cayman? Plus, why should I trust Carmine when he didn't trust me enough to let me help him look for Elijah?

No, I would keep this to myself for now. I had learned a lot on my own so far, and with Mikael and Scion's help, I might just get closer to finding Elijah than Carmine ever had.

"Are you ready?" Carmine asked, pointing his wand at my forehead as he stood.

"I'm ready," I said.

After screaming in pain for what felt like hours, I opened my eyes to see him gripping a piece of parchment from his desk, his knuckles turned white.

"Did you see anything?"

Carmine gritted his teeth, speaking through them. "Nothing useful. I just *know* there's something else that I'm missing here, something else connecting you and Elijah."

"But—"

Rip. Carmine had torn the rough parchment into two, which had to be hard to do.

"Did I do something wrong?"

Carmine sighed. "No, Jaden, you didn't. I'm just frustrated. You may return to class."

I left his office more confused than when I'd walked in.

CHAPTER TWENTY-THREE

I wanted answers. The frustration was just too much. I stumbled back to my room, closing the door behind me. Suddenly, a major idea sprang to my mind.

I grabbed Elijah's notebook from my pack and rummaged through it, the indecipherable, coded language the only thing meeting my gaze. Angry tears welled in my eyes as I stared at it.

"Come on," I said. My tears had made Elijah's note translate the first time. What if they could do the same for the notebook?

A tear fell down my face, splashing against a page in the middle. It tinged with fire, the same as when I had my Outburst. I tensed at the magic flowing over the page, connecting with the code words.

The door opened and Mikael stepped in. "What's going—"

"Shh," I whispered, pointing at the journal. "I think Elijah is sending me another message."

Mikael scrambled over and sat next to me on the floor as some of the code on the page swirled around, over and over, before transforming into one sentence:

I Will Appear To You Now

"Go get Scion!" I yelled.

Mikael ran out the door. It seemed to take forever for him to return. Sweat pooled on my forehead and fell into my eyes as I wrapped both hands around my wand. Mikael came back in the room, Scion in tow.

"What's going on?" she said.

Mikael showed her the journal entry.

"Elijah is coming?" The bedroom started to shake now, like we were in an earthquake. Everything on our bookshelves and walls fell to the bedroom floor with the force.

"Whoa," Mikael said. The shaking stopped as soon as it began.

"That's it?" I said.

"What do we do now?" Mikael said as I turned to them.

"Hand me that journal again," Scion said to me. "Something about the words there seemed . . . familiar to me."

"I thought you couldn't translate it," I said. "I don't think anyone knows this language but Elijah."

"He might be the only one that knows *all* of the words, but I know what this means," she said, pointing to a symbol below Elijah's one-sentence message.

"What?"

Scion pushed her braids behind her head, pointing at the symbol again. It was a simple fish illustration, colored in green. "It's Atlantean. It's the only one I understand. It means 'open the lost.'"

I touched the symbol with my wand. "Here goes nothing." I muttered the phrase. We yelped as the entire journal lit up with flames, causing us to drop it on the floor. An unearthly moan filled the bedroom, so loud that I was sure that everybody in the palace must have heard it. We put our hands over our ears as a ball of flame leaped into the air, the scream going silent.

We watched in awe as the flame elongated until familiar tennis shoes stepped out of the embers.

"Elijah?" I whispered, tears teeming in my eyes again. "Are you here?"

"It is Elijah," he said as he formed, the familiar smile wrapping his face. He looked the same, but different somehow, like he was shifting in and out. He turned to look at all three of us, winking in and out of existence. "Jaden, I see you've made friends here." His voice was Elijah's, but it sounded robotic, disembodied. Adult.

I sighed. "This isn't Elijah."

"It's a hologram," Scion said, awe seeping through her tone as she swept her hand through its body. "This is magic that I've seen before, but not from someone his age. Wow."

"Will it tell us what we need to know?" Mikael said.

"Yes," the hologram said, gesturing to us. "I'll need the final password though." It winked at me. "I can't just show you this without knowing if you're an enemy or not."

"I don't know the final password!" I said.

"Finish this sentence and I will reveal what I know," the Elijah hologram said. "'I know what I said 'cause . . .'"

"That's it?" Scion said, scrunching her eyebrows together. "How are we supposed to know the ending to *that*?"

Mikael shrugged. "I got nothing."

I gasped. I knew the answer to this one. "*I'm* the only one that's supposed to get this right. It's something my mama always says to me when I'm in trouble. We laughed about it all the time," I said, smiling at the hologram as I finished the saying. "'I was there when I said it!'"

"Precisely," the Elijah hologram said, smiling back at me.

The journal flew into the air, expanding until we could see the codes translating. Words bloomed across its pages before settling onto one page at the end. It contained one spell.

I pointed to it, my heart beating fast. It seemed like we were finally getting somewhere, finally getting the answers we deserved. "This has to be the research that Elijah showed Luxor in that vision I saw in Artwork!"

"My journal concludes on this page with this one spell, after I had completed my research into siphoning magic," hologram Elijah explained. "'Chọta mbinye aka anwansi' is the spell to find who is feeding themselves on others' magic. If you know where the magic is flowing, you'll find the evil."

I gripped my wand tight. "I'm ready to cast that spell."

"When you find the siphoner, we can fight the evil together, Jaden," the hologram said, sending a warm smile my way. "The entire universe depends on it."

He then winked out of existence, leaving us alone.

CHAPTER TWENTY-FOUR

"Chọta mbinye aka anwansi."

An orb bloomed from the bristlecone wand as I cast the spell later that night. Scion had stayed in our room until students went to sleep, and we had snuck out, casting Silence enchantments in our wake. Now, we stood at the top of the first-year staircase, too fearful to even move, as the orb floated in front of us.

"If Elijah's right, this will lead us to whoever's been siphoning magic and whoever caused the Ruin," I whispered. "We'll be catching Luxor in the act."

Mikael's warm hand squeezed my shoulder. "Are you sure you're ready for this? I mean . . . are we sure *any* of us are ready for this?"

I gripped my wand hard. "Ready as I'll ever be."

The orb floated down the stairs, and we followed it as it

disappeared underneath the door to the dungeons, settling at the underground pool.

"Why would it take us here?" Scion wondered. "This is where Genesis has her classes."

The orb floated toward a wall. A door appeared there, one I'd never seen before. We all stared at one another.

"Are we doing this?" Mikael said.

"We're doing this," I said.

But before we could reach for the handle, the door opened and a dark figure stepped out. We moved back in fear.

"We might need to call a professor," Mikael squeaked.

The figure stopped, jumping a bit, seeming startled to see us. Then it stepped out of the shadows.

It was Carmine.

We all gasped. As we watched, Carmine reached out to the floating orb, grabbed it, and shoved it into his mouth. He swallowed, moving his neck from left to right. "That always makes me feel good," he said, sighing loudly.

"Carmine?" I squeaked. "What . . . what's going on?"

He pointed his wand at me.

"Taking your magic, of course."

We screamed as an invisible tight cord squeezed around our waists and pulled us toward the door. The pain was so great my vision blurred, but I could just make out Carmine cackling to himself before jumping through the open doorway. We were pulled inside after him, a cacophony of unearthly growls and groans meeting us along with the grueling agony.

We landed on soft grass. The pain became too much to bear, and I could barely keep my food down. I heard my friends gasping hard, trying to catch their breaths. We lay in a clearing of sorts, a green stretch of land spreading around us, complete with trees, leaves, and a small cabin. An expansive night sky encircled us, bright stars twinkling, providing almost blinding light.

"This . . . this can't be right," Scion groaned. "Where . . . where are we?"

"Elijah disappeared because of Carmine?" Mikael asked. "That doesn't make any sense."

The door to the cabin opened, and Carmine took a step forward. "Oh, it makes the most sense. Who else could be powerful enough to come against a child with such robust magic like Elijah? He was so strong. That's why I started feeding on his magic. I was furious when he escaped, taking my source of strength with him. But . . . it seems like Jaden's magic is more potent than even his best friend's."

It all started to make horrible sense to me now. I stood, holding my wand aloft.

"What is this place?"

"My domain," Carmine said. "The place I've gone dormant in over the last thousand years. You asked me months ago how I've been alive for so long. I come here to rejuvenate after I siphon magic, entering a suspended state. This place allows me to keep living while I eat Wonder's magic."

"Why did you come get me when I had my Outburst?" I asked. "To gain my trust?"

"Oh, it's much more than that," Carmine said.

"That's why you wanted to study me, because you wanted to know how I got magic, because you wanted to find Elijah." I found myself getting angry as the full realization hit me. "It wasn't because you cared about me or him. You really wanted to—"

"Siphon his magic for yourself," Mikael finished for me, gasping in horror.

"*Tsk, tsk, tsk,*" Carmine said, taking another step forward. "Smart, but not smart enough. Jaden and Elijah's magic is special. When I drain the magic from normal children, it sustains me for a little while. But their magic . . . it will help me live forever without having to come here to rejuvenate." He didn't even wait for the horror to register on our faces before pointing his wand at Mikael and Scion. "Which makes you two useless."

"Run!" I yelled to them, but it was much too late.

"Kpochapu anwansi!"

Mikael and Scion fell unconscious immediately, floating in the air around me. Sparkles of golden light emitted from their mouths, and their throats bobbed up and down like they were choking, spitting out something housed deep inside them.

"It's their magic," Carmine answered for me. "I'll drain them of it *all* this time, and then they will die. Unless . . ."

"Let them go!" I screamed, clutching my wand tight, trying to figure out what I needed to do to defeat Carmine. But I was at a loss. I was still trying to deal with the fact that the person behind all of this was the man I had trusted from the beginning. All those times he had gone into my mind, all those times he had asked me about the circumstances surrounding my magic . . . it was all a plot.

"Unless you give me *your* magic, I'll be forced to kill them." Carmine's voice boomed over the clearing so loudly that the trees bent at the force of his tone. Wind flowed through the area, kicking up dust and leaves.

I decided to stall. "Why do you need my magic?"

Carmine walked so close that I could feel his breath on my face. "I know almost everything at The Five Emergences, Mr. Powers. I know you went to the library and researched. I didn't know *what* you found because the records disappear after you access them, but that tells me you know more about your Inheritance magic than you're letting on."

"My tears," I said. "They gave me my magic. Elijah gave me his magic, but . . . magic created me. It decided to create me."

Carmine took a step back. "You have more magic than you can imagine, Mr. Powers."

Tears welled in my eyes. "You never cared about Elijah."

He waved his hand dismissively. "No, I cared about him, but only because I wanted to siphon his magic for centuries. But, as you know, he slipped away from me. And that *fool*, Luxor, went after him. However, lo and behold, *you* showed up. Of course, I couldn't allow you to come to my school unless I knew everything about you. When you told me about your Outburst, I knew that I needed you way more than I ever needed Elijah."

"Why did you need me?"

Carmine drew himself to his full height, his face shifting a bit so that it looked skeletal. When I blinked, it returned to its usual brown. *What is going on?*

"Think about it. You know some of the answer." He opened his mouth; as he did, some of the sparkles surrounding Mikael and Scion poured inside him.

"Stop it!"

"I need the magic to sustain myself."

And then it hit me. I had asked him from the beginning about how he was still alive after a thousand years, why he hadn't intervened in human warfare and mayhem. And then another truth slammed into me. We only really saw him when he called me to his office for his sham investigations or when he broke up the fight between Silas and my friends. Other than that, he was never around.

Horror dawned on me. "Have you been . . . siphoning magic this entire time to keep yourself alive?"

"It's the only way I *can* stay alive. I must admit that I did start this school for talented students, but that all changed when the other founders died. I didn't want that for myself, so I had to create a curse that would allow me to take magic from others."

Carmine blinked, and when he moved, it was almost like he had turned into an old man. He limped closer to me. "But all of these students are so *weak*," he growled, rolling his eyes. "No, Wonder's magic can't sustain me for long; the Ruin will destroy it in due time, anyway. So, I go dormant throughout the year to keep my body from dying." He grabbed my face. Fire bloomed where he touched, and it felt like I was burning from the inside out. "That's why I needed Elijah. Someone like him could keep me alive for the next thousand years if I so chose."

"You. Won't. Take. My. Friend."

Carmine whispered a spell. We both lifted off the ground a few feet, his voice turning sinister. "You haven't been listening well enough, it seems. I just figured out that I don't *need* Elijah anymore now that I have you. I didn't know that he would disappear, but now I have the next best thing. He inadvertently caused magic to create *you*, to place both Inheritance magic and Love magic in you. Elijah is *nothing* compared to the power that your magic will offer me. I should have known it the moment the bristlecone wand bonded with you."

I struggled against the grip he had on me, but I could barely move.

"Cooperate and submit to be siphoned, and I'll let your friends live."

Carmine's mouth elongated, and I screamed in fear. It was like a dark cave existed inside him, huge and menacing. Light sparkles swirled around me as they lifted from me and traveled inside Carmine.

"No!" I said as I felt my life force drifting away. I still clutched the bristlecone wand and pushed outward in a last-ditch effort. Light blasted from it, and we flew in opposite directions, falling to the ground.

Before Carmine could recover, I cast ropes and wrapped

them around Carmine, pulling tight so that he couldn't escape. I ran over to the floating Mikael and Scion as he yelled behind me, struggling against the dirt.

"Wake up, wake up, wake up," I said, shaking their shoulders and faces. "Please, wake up." I didn't know what else to do; the curse they were under was connected to Carmine, so I had no clue how to get them back to safety without him releasing them.

Whoosh. I turned to see Carmine lifting off the ground, the ropes absorbing into his body as he groaned. He smiled at me. "You're going to have to try much harder than that."

With a slice of his wand, balls of fire flew through the air, barreling toward me. I managed to dodge most of them as I ran, but not all. One hit the ground, a crater appearing in the dirt. I fell and my pant leg caught fire. I cried out as I sat up, dousing it with water from my wand as the material broke apart. Carmine's foot appeared on my chest, pinning me down.

He ground his foot, and I cried out, gasping for breath.

"Give me your magic, Jaden. There's *no* escape." Sparkles flew around me again as Carmine opened his mouth to suck the magic from me. "I promise to keep you alive while I do it . . ."

I lay there, gasping for breath as wind flowed through the clearing, doing my best to struggle against Carmine's strength, but I realized I could do nothing else. I did my best to just relax, to let it all go. It was all I could do now. The sparkles swirled all over me, to the point where I could see nothing but Carmine's boot on my chest. I waited for the darkness to consume me, to give me the peace I had wanted since Elijah had disappeared. Maybe it wasn't all so bad, to finally give up, to let all the stress go. A serenity settled on my shoulders as I stopped gasping for breath and closed my eyes.

But there was also something else there, a *fire* in my soul that bloomed inside me. *In spite* of me.

You need to get up. I did this for a reason.

What was that? Who was that?

Use what I have given you. Do you want to beat Carmine?

I did want to beat him, more than anything in both worlds.

Then. Get. Up. Now!

With all my strength, I opened my eyes. Carmine removed his boot from my chest and kicked my wand away from me. His face appeared in the sparkles, smiling at me as his foot returned to my chest. "You won't need that where you're going, Mr. Powers."

The fire roared in me, raging out of control. It was like a switch had been turned on, and I felt immense power. The same as I felt in the underground pool with Silas. I wasn't going to let Carmine use me for his schemes. With a roar I pushed his foot off me and twisted it with a sickening *crunch*. Carmine yelped in pain as I stood, pointing his wand at me. But it was way too late for him to stop me now.

I raised both of my hands by instinct. Where it came from, I didn't know. An orb of swirling energy pooled in between my fingertips as the four of us were lifted by an invisible force. We flew through the air, out of the clearing and out of the doorway, back to the palace's underground pool.

"Mr. Powers!" Professor Menifee screamed from near the pool's edge. She was flanked by Professor Genesis.

Carmine screamed, lunging at me with his mouth agape.

With a grunt, I threw the orb of energy at Carmine. It exploded as it connected with his chest, sending him flying across the room, his head clunking against the opposite wall. The orb buried itself in his chest as he screamed, thick chains wrapping around him.

It was all chaos after that. Menifee raced toward me with her wand raised, Genesis following close behind her as Carmine continued to scream at and curse me. Mikael and Scion woke up, looking bewildered at the entire scene. And there was me, my hands sparkling with dark energy.

"The underground pool alerted me to students being out past curfew," Genesis said, stumbling over to us. She glared at Mikael and Scion. "I thought the Ruin was now inside the building, so I got Menifee to assist."

Even with the powerful magic I now possessed, I felt incomplete. I thrust my left hand outward, and the bristlecone wand flew through a blue haze from what seemed like nowhere and back to me, safe and sound.

"He tried to kill me!" I yelled at Menifee. "He's the actual siphoner! It's why Elijah disappeared!"

Menifee aimed her wand at Carmine and glanced at Genesis. "Make sure every student is locked inside their bedrooms until further notice." She nodded to me. "Everyone except you."

I gestured to Mikael and Scion. "Not without them. They know everything I know."

"Very well."

Carmine moaned from his prison. "This isn't over! I'll get what I want! You just wait and see!" The light from the orb encircled him. It sank into his body until it was absorbed. Then he disappeared in a flash of flames.

"Where did he go?" I screamed, running over to where I had held him captive. "He was just here!"

A scared Genesis cast an anxious glance Menifee's way as she ran out of the dungeons. "I'll take care of the students, Cinxia."

Menifee turned to me. "I believe you, but I need answers and I need them *now*, Mr. Powers."

CHAPTER TWENTY-FIVE

The familiar row houses of Columbia Heights greeted me as I made my way back home, after traveling via Puddle. I had to call my parents from downtown near a bookstore because it was the only place that had a residual puddle from a previous rainstorm. It hadn't rained in DC in days.

Fall break had come early to The Five Emergences, after everything that had happened with Carmine. After he had fled, the students were put on lockdown for a few days, meals delivered to them until the professors could guarantee safe passage back home for everyone.

And then the real work began, with trying to unravel what had happened in conversation with Professor Menifee and the other professors. They'd sat in awe and disbelief as we told them the entire story, doing our best to keep my Inheritance magic secret. That didn't last long, considering that Menifee and Genesis had seen the orb between my hands and had seen my wand return to me *after* I had already used magic on Carmine to defeat him. After questioning us for days, they had let us go, and then they made Menifee the interim Headmaster until the school year was over.

"Make sure you stay vigilant over break," Menifee had told me as she walked me to the Puddle that would take me home. "The protective spells we've cast over your home should hold against Carmine if he decides to come for you."

"Will you be looking for him?"

Menifee had stared intensely at me. "As long as I'm the head of this school, he's priority number one."

Now, though, I sat in Dad's SUV after he picked me up from the bookstore, expertly weaving in and out of traffic.

"You sure you want to go back in the new year?" He glanced at me in the rearview mirror. Mom sat next to him. Menifee had kept all parents updated on the situation after we went into lockdown. "We sure could use you around the house, especially with Austin. He misses his brother."

I twirled my wand. "Nah, I wanna go back. It's like a second home to me now."

"I just can't believe all of this has happened," Mama said.

Pride soared in me as I thought about Elijah. "I'm just glad that Elijah's still alive out there. Somewhere."

"He would be so proud of you."

Because he knew I could handle it. I missed him terribly, and he probably knew that too, which was why our love for each other created this magic inside me. Magic I still didn't really understand. I had learned over the last few months that magic was its own thing, its own *energy* that could do what it wanted, when it wanted. I was just glad that it had chosen me for this mission. Now, I just hoped that the professors would put all their resources into finding Elijah and Luxor.

I still wasn't sure why Elijah and Luxor hadn't returned after Carmine had been exposed. After *I* had exposed Carmine.

Even now as we pulled into our driveway, I felt the Inheritance magic coursing in my veins, beating something powerful. I felt . . . different ever since I had used it and made it my own.

Dad helped me out of the car, picking up my bags and carrying them into the house with Mama. I stepped inside. Looking around my home felt familiar, like I had been missing a part of me since going to magic school. After sighing once, I headed upstairs to my room where Dad had placed my belongings.

I was still lonely. I had met Mikael and Scion and had fought an evil I barely understood, but I did it all without Elijah, without my best friend. How in the world was I supposed to deal with everything when he was gone?

"Why haven't you come back, Elijah?" I asked aloud as I sat on my bed. "There's no need for you to keep hiding. Come back to us."

Nothing happened, not like I was expecting it to. Maybe he was content with where he was. Maybe he was traveling the known and unknown worlds with Luxor and couldn't care less about everything I'd accomplished in his absence.

I tossed my wand from hand to hand before opening my bottomless pack and pulling out Elijah's spiral notebook. I knew now that my tears meant magic, that they meant *him*. It wasn't hard to cry when I wanted to be close to him again.

I needed him.

Water leaked from my eyes, hitting one of the pages.

Gold light shone in the droplets, causing me to sit back, my eyes widening. It was happening again, just like I knew it would. Words wrote on the page:

I'm always here for you.

The tears congealed into one glob, which dripped to the floor of its own accord. A shimmering figure grew upward, and I gasped and held a hand to my mouth so I wouldn't scream.

The figure laughed a familiar laugh as it stepped forward. "Hey, bighead. Wassup?"

"Elijah?" I said, tears welling in my eyes again. "Is that you? Are you really here?"

"Yes, it's me, silly," he said. "I'm here, and I'm not an illusion, vision, memory, or hologram. It's me." It *was* him, the boy I remembered, my best friend. He was solid, and he wasn't casting himself into my bedroom from some far-off place. No, he was my real best friend, the Elijah with the dark skin and slanted nose and playful eyes.

I crushed myself against him, folding both arms around him. His arms came up at the same time and held me tightly against him. I heard him breathing and heard his heart beating. That place in my own heart that had disappeared when they had told me he had died was returning, healing like it had never been hurt, had never been destroyed. I took a deep breath, and the unmistakable scent of his favorite soap filled my nose.

"Are you . . . are you okay?" I said when we finally pulled apart from each other.

He knelt before me as I sat on my bed again, and put a hand to my cheeks, wiping my tears away. "Oh, Jaden. I should be asking you that same question. Are *you* okay? I can't believe I let you get involved in this, get involved in all this danger. I am so sorry. I just didn't know who else to tell about everything. Can you ever forgive me? I didn't know you would get magic. I just hoped you could get someone to help me."

I touched his hand, feeling the pressure of it on my cheek. He was so real, so *here*. It was the best feeling ever. "Of course, I forgive you. I've become a Sorcerer because of you getting your notebook over to me."

He smiled sheepishly. "I'm so happy you are one. Now we have even more in common."

My tone turned serious. "I'm glad you're here. I can't go through this alone."

"I'm here, Jaden. And you were never alone. I've been watching you from afar all of this time, tracking your movements.

I know everything you've done." His hand slipped from my cheek.

"Then you know I found out about Carmine."

Disgust stretched across his face as he grimaced. "Even I didn't know it was him at first. But, there's no greater evil than Carmine. Believe me when I tell you. By now you know that Professor Luxor was my academic adviser and that he set off to find me when he heard the explosion in Carmine's office."

I grew a little embarrassed. "I mean, we thought it was Luxor siphoning magic at first. But then your hologram gave us the magic signatures spell. If you hadn't, we wouldn't have found out it was Carmine."

He nodded. "I was smart enough to know that something else was going on. I built a lab at The Five Emergences, so I started doing experiments on the school's campus under the cover of night. I found that the magic signatures at the palace didn't correlate with the ones emanating from greater Wonder. I knew I had to get out of there after Carmine put me into that enchanted sleep. Luxor found me, and we knew he would come for us next, to eat our magic completely and kill us to protect his secret."

"Well, that's over." I clutched his hand, and he twirled his fingers in mine. "We can fight Carmine together."

"There's still things Luxor, you, and I need to do." His eyes took on a hint of mystery as he continued. "We have to figure out *why* you have magic. We know the *how* now, thanks to you, but we need to know more."

"What are you saying? I thought it was to fight Carmine."

"We think there's more to it. Professor Hadiza says that magic has a mind of its own, right? Well, we think we have some leads as to where it actually is. We are doing our best to find its source."

I leaned forward. "You mean to tell me that magic is actually . . . a person?"

He shook his head. "Not a person, exactly. But a living thing. And it made a decision for a reason. Not only did it create Inheritance magic in you, but it also made me smarter and faster years ago, able to do feats of magic that even adults haven't mastered. We need to find it for the fight ahead."

I thought about the voice I'd heard in my head when I'd fought Carmine. "It . . . it *is* a living thing. It made me fight back, made me remember that it had given me this magic for a reason."

His eyebrow lifted. "I *knew* it. You have a connection to it. Will you come with us and help us?"

I reached out for a fist bump. "Heck yeah!"

"You have to know that Carmine is more powerful than you all give him credit for. You've weakened him, but that doesn't mean he will stay that way. The Ruin will only grow larger. He feeds off magic, Jaden. Wonder *is* magic, which means he won't stay down for long."

"What do you need me to do?"

Soft wind started to flow into my bedroom from the open window. "We will go back to school after fall break. I'll teach you as much magic as I know, and then we will try to find the curse Carmine created that turned him into what he is now. We need to reverse the magic somehow to kill him and destroy the Ruin for good. Finally, we need to find magic itself and learn why it made you this way and why it gave me my Outburst at four. We were chosen for this, both of us."

I thrust my wand forward. "Let's do this!"

He stood, let go of my hand, and planted a kiss on my forehead before pointing at his notebook. "The words have all been translated now."

"We can do this; I know we can."

He sent me that playful Elijah smile he was known for. "But first, we deserve a break, now that I'm out of hiding! We can sleep and play basketball and eat . . . and eat . . . and eat some more. And play basketball . . ."

"And eat some more!"

I grabbed his hand, and we ran downstairs and out the front door, all the way to his parents' house, where we dribbled and dunked the basketball for the next few hours.

I won as many games as he did this time.

And I wouldn't have had it any other way.

ACKNOWLEDGMENTS

Writing this book has been nothing but a dream come true for me. As a young child in middle school, I stayed in the library. It was my safe space, my place to deal with the chaotic world I was born into. I used to love getting off the bus in the morning and heading to the library to read, sometimes missing breakfast. Ms. Fisher and Ms. Heller were my middle school librarians and transferred to high school with me. That time in my life was very hard for me, but books became my escape, and my love for middle grade novels was born then. I loved everything about reading as a child, and that love has inspired every novel that I have ever written.

I first want to thank Ms. Fisher and Ms. Heller, my childhood librarians. We didn't have many librarians in our neighborhood, so school was the first place where I was able to foster my love of reading through Ms. Fisher's and Ms. Heller's love of reading. Both of you recognized me as a strong reader and would always give me suggestions on what to read next. Ms. Heller, I still remember you coming to my classroom and handing me books that you knew I wanted to read, saving multiple trips to the library. Ms. Fisher, I still remember you putting holds on the upcoming books that were coming to the library so that I would be the first one to read them. Both of you were my first inspirations—I haven't found you both yet since I have moved away from my little town, but I cannot wait to gift this book to you when I meet you again.

To Caitie Flum, thank you for seeing the potential in this book from the beginning and helping me to get it published.

To Mary Kate Castellani, thank you for seeing the promise of this book before it was even written. You helped to get this book in the world just by reading a paragraph synopsis and helping to shepherd it through the offices at Bloomsbury to get it published.

To Camille Kellogg—you are the toughest editor I've *ever* worked with. Thank you for not allowing me to turn in something that wasn't publishable. Thank you for making me write, edit, revise, write some more, delete whole passages, and then write some more. This book wouldn't be in the spot it is in now if not for you.

Finally, I'd like to talk to my inner child, that child that needed help, that child that just wanted everything to be all right. I want you to know that one day you'll be on the journey to being okay. It's going to be a hard fight because you will have to go through all of the emotions of life on your own, but you'll get there. I love you. And the world loves you and your words, too.